Also from Robert Barnard

A
Charitable
Body

ROBERT BARNARD

SCRIBNER

NEW YORK   LONDON   TORONTO   SYDNEY   NEW DELHI

SCRIBNER

A Division of Simon & Schuster, Inc.
1230 Avenue of the Americas
New York, NY 10020

First Scribner hardcover edition January 2012

SCRIBNER and design are registered trademarks of The Gale Group, Inc., used under license by Simon & Schuster, Inc., the publisher of this work.

For information about special discounts for bulk purchases, please contact Simon & Schuster Special Sales at 1-866-506-1949 or business@simonandschuster.com.

The Simon & Schuster Speakers Bureau can bring authors to your live event. For more information or to book an event, contact the Simon & Schuster Speakers Bureau at 1-866-248-3049 or visit our website at www.simonspeakers.com.

Manufactured in the United States of America

10 9 8 7 6 5 4 3 2 1

ISBN 978-1-4391-7744-0

A
Charitable
Body

CHAPTER 1

Change of Life

※

"Very nice," said Rupert Fiennes, licking his tongue delicately around his lips. "Boiled is easily my favorite way of having an egg."

"The easiest, anyway," said his cousin Mary-Elizabeth rather grimly, as was her wont whenever anything even remotely connected to their new and only comparative penury came up. "Mrs. Tower always said it was a very poor sort of breakfast."

"Oh, Mrs. Tower was devoted to bacon and sausages, to mushrooms and black pudding," said Rupert. "We had to have them because she enjoyed them herself. I always hated piled-high breakfasts in the army, and I hoped for something simpler when I got out. Croissants, maybe, or cold meats and cheeses. As so often, Walbrook Manor defeated me."

"Don't be disrespectful of Walbrook. You know it pains me to the heart that we have lost it."

"It doesn't pain me to the heart, but I'll try to be silent in my rejoicings in future."

They were just finishing the washing-up when Mary-Elizabeth looked at her watch.

"Oh goody! There's time to read the papers. I haven't got to be at the vicarage until eleven o'clock."

"Now you see what a wonderful thing running hot water is," said Rupert. "You'd still be waiting for the kettle to boil if we were living at Walbrook Manor."

Mary-Elizabeth said nothing. That was always the way to get the best of Rupert. She settled down to the bits and pieces in the *Times'* Arts supplement and was well advanced with the sudoku when she checked her watch again and then hurried into the hall and put on her outdoor coat.

"Ah, Mary. Just a word before you go," said her cousin, coming out from his study. He didn't speak to her as a cousin, much more like a brother, which is how she regarded him. "Got all your papers for your meeting read and digested?" he temporized.

"We don't have much paperwork in the Women's Institute committee. Now what is it, Rupert?"

"I've been thinking—it troubled me—about your sorrow at losing Walbrook."

"Well, don't. Really, Rupert—"

"I think sometimes you throw a pretty pink halo around the place, forgetting how horribly inconvenient it was."

"I am quite aware of that. I have reason to be."

"Of course you do. But I was wondering, would you like a position—well, a job, to be frank—in Walbrook when the place is really open to the public on a full-time basis?"

A smile burst onto Mary-Elizabeth's usually rather glum face.

"I can think of nothing I'd like better. But be careful, Rupert. The other members of the Walbrook Trust Board might condemn you as wanting to keep control even when you've handed the house over to them. No—there's no *might* about it: some of them certainly would."

"I'm aware of that. I will go very carefully. And you must go carefully and not try to glamorize the place's past. There were very ugly sides to the days when our family ran the manor and almost everything around it. The Trust, quite rightly, would expect a degree of balance in how the house's history is presented to the public."

"And they'd get it from me. I *do* appreciate how much easier life is in this flat. Everything works, everything is convenient and saves us no end of trouble. We can concentrate on what interests us, not on the grind of everyday living. So in many ways we're both better off than we were."

"Of course we are. I knew you must see that," said Rupert, his relief showing in his voice.

"Still, this place is a bit lacking in style, history, people's loves and struggles and dilemmas, isn't it?"

With that Mary-Elizabeth made her way out of the front door, being careful not to bang it.

A few minutes later Rupert passed his cousin as she was gazing into the window of Mrs. Borden's secondhand-book shop (OPEN THURSDAYS AND SATURDAY MORNINGS the sign said), and he stopped and

3

broached to her what he had been thinking on his walk.

"You know, I wonder whether instead of a job it wouldn't be easier to get you into one of the vacant places on the Trust Board. No payment involved—but we can't pretend we are in need of money."

"No . . . a place on the board sounds glorious, Rupert. We'd make a great team."

"Ah . . ." Rupert gave every appearance of having been caught out. "I was thinking instead of me, not in addition to," he said, and resumed his walk to the manor.

That was typical of Rupert, his cousin thought. He floated ideas, then shut down any discussion of them, assuming that he, and his interlocutor, needed time to sort things out in their own minds. It was a surprisingly effective way of proceeding. But this time he momentarily turned back.

"The meeting today is going to discuss the matter of the rolling exhibitions on the first floor. At the moment the plan is for a new exhibition each year, with a wide range of topics."

"I'd support that," said Mary-Elizabeth. "*Some*thing is needed to get the crowds in."

"The choice for the first exhibition is between one on the First World War and its poets and one on our great queen consorts."

Mary-Elizabeth thought for a few seconds.

"Well, you know me: I'm a glutton for royal. But not for the first exhibition. Not serious enough. How can you be a *great* queen consort? And people won't lend their royal pictures to an untried organization. I'd back the war poets. Pathos and tragedy, and the odd story of heroism. And you'd get lots of school parties. It would get Walbrook's education department off to a good start when it is finally put together."

Rupert nodded and went on his way. He was impressed by his cousin's grasp of practicalities. She would make a much better representative of the family on the board than he did. And it would give him, finally, freedom from the burden of Walbrook. It was something "devoutly to be wished"—had been for more than twenty years.

The lawn sloped gently down to the river, with, dotted around, a shrub pretending it had grown there quite casually. Felicity would have liked to play games with Thomas—let go of the pram and then chase it, then repeat the joke. But Thomas was a serious baby and could carry for life the conviction that his mother was a potential infanticide. Quite enough crime in the Peace household, thank you. Felicity turned back into the weed-covered rose garden, enjoying a rather tentative second flowering, and then round toward the front of the house and the main entrance.

From here the old manor house looked its best, with its plethora of windows regularly reflecting the Yorkshire sun, and Felicity was longing to go inside to see whether the interior was similarly welcoming and well planned. The early-eighteenth-century builder who had designed and delivered this house to its first owner must have had a modicum of sheer genius in his makeup.

The notice said HOUSE OPEN TUESDAY AND SATURDAY

MORNINGS. Today was Saturday, the time was eleven o'clock, but when she tried to enter, she was politely told that she could not take Thomas.

"But I thought there was some kind of crèche for young children," she said.

"Oh, there is," said the woman with an all-purpose smile, "but only for the Tuesday openings and bank holidays. That's not very convenient for families we know, but the fact is we can't get volunteers to staff the crèche on Saturdays."

"I see. I guess you're really just testing the waters at the moment, aren't you?"

"We are. The house is run by a charitable trust, and the people on the governing body all donate their time. Do come back some Tuesday. Or bring your husband."

Felicity had to fight the suspicion that the woman saw that her husband was black (not difficult by looking at Thomas), and she assumed that he would therefore not be interested in the treasures of Walbrook Manor and could be left to mind the baby. No point in rummaging round for possible prejudices though. And at least the woman had presumed a father was in the picture. Felicity smiled and said she was sure there was plenty to see in the garden.

She continued walking, just to familiarize herself with the setup. She knew an herb garden had once been here, and a wildflower meadow, but from that point between the manor and the car park most of what she could see was still lawn and hedgerow, and the drive leading to the main road. Some way from the main gates was a substantial block that her little guide to the estate identified as the stables—no longer used for horses obviously, and with a long, windowed extension. Certainly it was now used for something else, because cars were arriving and turning into a small, special parking area.

Felicity watched, idly, as people walked toward the main entrance to the stables. Some smart, country people, some more scruffy ones; men in open-necked shirts, broad-beamed women in slacks. One young woman got off a bus outside the gates with a buggy and pushed her baby toward the meeting or social get-together that was obviously scheduled to go on. Felicity watched her, and a man who came out from a side door to the manor and started in the direction of the stables—a slim, elderly figure, impeccably dressed in dark-gray suiting, with a good head of hair, and a way of walking that gave Felicity the idea of someone walking on water. She wondered if he could be the person in charge of the museum-to-be—director, curator, or whatever. Perhaps chairman of the Trust.

Felicity had all the time in the world before Carola, her elder child, would be finished for the day at her riding school. She decided she would wander toward the stables later and then go and find the wildflower meadow if it still existed. More to the point at the moment, which her watch showed to be close to eleven thirty, was to go to the little cafeteria that she had seen on the other side of the manor and get herself a cup of coffee and maybe a cream bun. Felicity was one of those people, almost unnatural people it was often thought, who never had to watch their weight. She had settled Thomas with a rattle in an otherwise empty café (one offering good coffee and basic cakes and biscuits obviously supplied by a local bakery chain) and was enjoying a leisurely snack when the door opened again and another woman came in—one in a similar position to herself: child in a baby buggy and a need for coffee, which she fetched from the counter before settling into a nearby table with an outlook on the sloping grass. It was the woman who had got off the bus and whom Felicity had last seen going toward the meeting. She was crying.

Tears were rolling down her cheeks, her light makeup was smudged, and when she had had a couple of sips from her cup, she put her head on the table and Felicity heard gulps of anger or frustration.

"Can I help?" Felicity asked, getting up and going over to her. For a moment there was no reply. "I think I saw you arriving at the stables a little while ago. Is there something wrong?"

The woman looked up.

"I don't see how you can," she said, thrusting out her hand. "I'm Maya Tyndale."

"I'm Felicity Peace."

"It's nice of you, but I don't think you can help. I may be being silly. It's those bastards in there."

"What bastards? In the stables?"

"Yes. It's a meeting of the Walbrook Manor Trust Board. The trustees of this place, of whom I am one, fool that I am. I just feel so *frustrated*. They took me for a fool, and I was a fool."

And she told Felicity all about it.

*　　*　　*

8

When Maya had arrived at the Trustees' Room in the stable block, things seemed to be going on pretty much as normal.

"Ah, good to see you again, er, Maya," said Sir Stafford Quarles, as usual pronouncing her name *Meyer* and sounding as if he were welcoming a regular guest at his upmarket B and B.

"And is this little Feo?" asked Mattie Fowler, bundled up in the weirdest assortment of clothes. "Feisty little bugger I wouldn't mind betting, eh?"

Maya smiled. "Yes, this is Theo. I'm still breast-feeding him. People say it's the thing to do, though I'm not sure I'd do it a second time."

All as per regular form, then. But as Maya took her coffee and biscuit and settled down in a chair with Theo watching her from his stroller with his inquiring gaze, she had a strong sense that things were not as normal. Why was Mrs. Porritt avoiding eye contact, though she had always come up to greet Maya before? Why did the little group of three in the far corner of the room keep half looking round in her direction, then sharply turning away again?

"We must have a talk about that exhibition you have in mind, er, Maya," said Sir Stafford as he passed her by in search of more highly regarded prey. He floated on air from soul to soul, with an encouraging nod for all of them. He had been holding out to Maya the prospect of a small exhibition in the Garden Room at the time of the next Walbrook Festival, and Maya had a series of lithographs inspired by the house and gardens that she longed to see hung there. She had talked to Wesley Gannett, the museum director, and he had said it was a good idea, but Sir Stafford had never mentioned it to him. If it was to be part of the festival that was Sir Stafford's remit, not Gannett's. It had been agreed that the trustees would virtually take over the house for those two weeks.

"Er, I think we could . . . ," said Sir Stafford, his voice slightly raised from its normal murmur. Everyone became quiet, perhaps because of his title, perhaps because he alone of the trustees had an intimate connection with museums and galleries, having spent most of his working life running them. They all began taking their places round the table, apparently at random, in fact guided by a series of alliances that Maya was only just beginning to fathom.

"I've called for this, er, private session of the board because we, er—"

But he was interrupted, almost as if according to plan.

"Chairman, if I could just make a point before we begin," said Mrs. Porritt, her face set in a stern, judicial mask, as if she were about to rummage in her handbag and pull out a black cap.

"Yes, er, Janet, of course."

"It is clear in the Articles of Association that the board consists of those elected to it and those co-opted onto it. Anyone not a member of the Board of Trustees can only be invited to attend its meetings, usually for a particular item on its agenda, except for the director of the museum." The face had gained an accretion of granite. "There is a person here who is not a member of the board and who has not been invited."

Several members looked at Theo, or at the handles of his pram, he being sunk beneath the tabletop. Other members stared down at their agenda and minutes of the last meeting.

Maya's mouth almost dropped open with astonishment. "You must be joking!"

"Now, er, Maya, I'm sure if you think about it, you will understand," mumbled Sir Stafford. "There are rules in the Articles—"

"But I asked you when I came to the Festival Committee, told you I couldn't get a minder for this date, and I'd have to bring Theo. You said everyone would understand since most of them had 'been there themselves.'"

"Ah," said Sir Stafford, "I think there has been a slight misunderstanding. I couldn't preempt a decision of the board—"

"But Theo isn't a person! He's only eight months old!"

"I think you will find that there is no lower age limit to being a person. Certainly the Articles of Association stipulate none. I think for him to remain we need a motion. I propose that the motion reads, 'That Theo Tyndale be allowed to attend this meeting.' Do I have a proposer? A seconder? Excellent. Those for the motion—"

Maya was getting her things together almost before the vote was complete. There were six for, then six against, the latter vote including Sir Stafford's. When he gave his casting vote, Theo was certified as a noninvited person and Maya took hold of the baby buggy, not even trying to suppress her outrage, and marched him out of the boardroom. The comic aspects of the self-important body declining to have a baby observe its proceedings did not strike her till later. Her overwhelming feeling was that she had been outmaneuvered.

"In what sense outmaneuvered?" asked Felicity. "And what were they trying to achieve?"

"I don't *know*," replied Maya. "But the private session of the board is going to be a discussion of Wes Gannett's future with us. That's what they'll be doing now. He's the museum director, and his initial contract is nearly up. I think they calculated who would vote for him to continue, and who would be against. I'd been sounded out at a committee meeting and I was very much in favor of a renewed contract. I presume I've been got rid of so as to have a clear vote not to renew the contract. Much more satisfactory than having to use the chairman's casting vote. That always smells of a fit-up—one person having two votes."

"A fit-up, as you've been fitted up," said Felicity.

"Exactly. I was also in favor of having a permanent exhibition in the house rather than a series of less ambitious ones."

"Less ambitious ones?"

"I wanted a big subject: a history of the women's movement, in fact."

"Ah. Not the best time for it. Either twenty years late or I would guess twenty years before its time."

"Maybe. Anyway I had some support but by no means enough."

"Now Gannett: why do half the board want to sack him?"

"Search me. But I'm pretty sure the chairman does.

That's Sir Stafford Quarles. He's managed, as he usually does, to get half the board on his side."

"Sir Stafford being the chairman," said Felicity meditatively. "And to do that he had to get rid of you?"

Maya nodded. "I'm just an art teacher and part-time artist."

"And they'll still be discussing it?"

Maya peered out of the window in the direction of the stable block.

"Wesley isn't pacing around outside but I think they allotted an hour to the discussion, so they probably haven't voted on him yet. They are capable of having an hour's discussion on whether to dispense with having biscuits with the tea or coffee, so they surely can have an hour on a genuinely important topic."

"Then why don't you go back to the meeting?" Felicity asked. "You might be in time for the vote. I can look after Theo."

Maya looked at her. "Oh, but I couldn't. Two babies, two prams—"

"Theo looks to be a lot less trouble than Carola, my eldest, when she was young. Go on—I'll finish my coffee and bun and then take a walk outside. Get along—hurry. Take all the time you need in there."

Maya looked at Felicity questioningly, got an encouraging nod, then dashed out of the cafeteria and hurried through the wilting rose garden in the direction of the old stables.

Maya paused for a moment, then opened the door of the Trustees' Room.

"Problem solved," she said brightly. More brightly than she actually felt. She shot a glance around the table. Janet Porritt was obviously trying to think up a point of order or remember some obscure clause in the Articles of Association. Sir Stafford was clearly—a rare occurrence—nonplussed.

"Ah, I see. You've not—"

"I haven't left him in a basket by the bulrushes," said Maya. "Or palmed him off on one of our members of staff. He's being looked after—thank you for your concern."

Her carefree tone obviously brought Sir Stafford up short. "Ah—splendid. We've not managed to come to any decision." He obviously had tried to drain any sign of regret from his voice but had failed. Maya had returned to the meeting just in time.

"I have to say I don't yet see why some members are unwilling to renew the contract," said Ben Hooley, a local primary-school head teacher. "Gannett may have taken time to settle in, but this was his first job in this kind of organization—"

"Australia," murmured Sir Stafford. "How should he have had experience of a fine house such as Walbrook?"

"But it's good sometimes to get an entirely outside view of things, don't you think? Anyway, the point I'm making is that since he recovered from the death of his wife, he's been a first-rate director in my view. Absolutely on the ball as far as his ideas on presentation are concerned, with real expertise in eighteenth- and nineteenth-century art, which is where we need it. He did a wonderful job in his paper on pensions, absolutely on top of all the legislation about disabled access—really an all-round man, and a great success."

"I'd agree with that," said Maya. "You've only got to look at the visitor numbers, even though we're only open two days a week, all the wonderful publicity we've had, and the take-up for the education program starting next year—it's fantastic."

Sir Stafford had sucked in a very audible breath. "I think visitor numbers have everything to do with social trends and very little to do with the business of a director."

"There is a danger," said Maya quietly, "that whenever something is going wrong the fault lies with the director, and whenever it is going right, it is not his achievement."

"Particularly," said Ben Hooley, "remembering something that no one is mentioning, though it is highly relevant: the fact that the previous director was suspended and then got rid of after only six months. What is it going to do to our reputation if another director falls by the wayside?"

There was instant babble, with one-half of the board shouting and wagging fingers at the other half. The most interesting exchange that Maya could distinguish was "The complaint from the members of staff was absolutely unanimous" and the comment "That is what most people found suspicious."

Maya decided, as a newish member of the board, that she should try to act as peacemaker.

"If I may make a suggestion," she said. A sheepish

quiet fell over the room, but several looked at her with open hostility on their faces. "There seem to be two opinions on whether Wes has been a success as director or not. We need to acknowledge both views. But there can be no two opinions about the likelihood of damaging publicity—certainly in the local papers, possibly in the national ones as well. We must remember that the more successful the festival is, the more we are the object of general interest. I suggest we reach a compromise: that Wes's contract be renewed for a further two years."

It wasn't what Sir Stafford wanted, but he had been stymied by the threat of damaging publicity.

"*One* year?" he suggested almost timidly.

"If he has only one year, he will spend much of his time applying for jobs," said Maya. "We won't get the best out of him."

"Agreed," said Ben Hooley. "And Wes's best is very good."

"And we can use the current financial situation—practically every museum and gallery in the land is feeling the pinch these days, with the American visitor numbers so poor—to explain why we can't do more at the moment," said Maya.

In the event, the compromise was passed on the nod. By now Wes Gannett was waiting in the sun outside, and he was called to the meeting, no longer private, and the discussion went on its rambling, inconsequential way. Maya, moderately happy at the outcome, stayed to the end.

*   *   *

In the late-autumn sunlight Felicity did a great deal of wheeling up and down and round about, becoming quite dextrous at coping with one baby buggy in each hand. She did a bit of elementary playing with Theo, though he was inclined to roll himself up into a ball and gurgle. She kept an eye on the house. The small but steady stream of visitors included several carrying musical instruments. Most of the paying customers came for their stroll around after their visit to the house, though not the musicians.

From the open windows of one of the downstairs rooms, Felicity heard a series of chamber pieces and thought this added a distinct plus to her visit. When she saw an elderly man being wheeled by a young woman out of the lodge just outside the main gates and proceeding toward the house, she recognized the composer Graham Quarles—he must be the brother, cousin, or at any rate some relation to Sir Stafford Quarles, the chairman of the board, whom Maya Tyndale had mentioned. Graham, after a period of eclipse during the era of twelve-tone music and outré experiments with percussive utensils, was enjoying something of a revival. She had recently read a piece about him in one of the Sunday papers. As the man in the wheelchair neared the house and he heard the music being rehearsed inside, his right hand began making little gestures, as if in response to the music. His left side and hand were inert, lifeless, and she realized he had probably suffered a stroke.

She walked toward him to get as unobtrusively as possible a better look, but at that moment the main door into the stables opened and the members of the board emerged, their meeting over. Most of them got into their cars and drove away, and only Maya Tyndale headed in the direction of the house.

"Did it go well?" asked Felicity, as Maya took over her buggy and they walked together up to the house.

"Pretty well." Maya looked at the house, red and inviting in the sunlight. But she shook her head, declining its invitation. "Have you got a car?"

"In the main car park here."

"I feel like talking, but not around the house. Would that be an imposition?"

"Not at all. I'm curious. I'm always curious, in fact. Would a pub be okay? I'm not breast-feeding and I feel like a long drink."

"Perfect. I am, but I actually like orange juice. Can we manage two strong-willed males and two strollers?"

"With difficulty, but it can be done."

So half an hour later they were in the Black Heifer in Kettlestone drinking orange juice and a small lager, and Maya was recounting the events of the meeting in a purely factual way, as Felicity had suggested would be the best. She was interested first in information, only later in conjecture or impression.

"So," she said, as Maya finished, "the director has two further years. Was that why I didn't see Sir Stafford come out at the end of the meeting? He was talking with Wesley Gannett about the board's decision?"

"That's right," said Maya with a grimace.

"Having kept him on tenterhooks throughout the main part of the meeting?"

"Right again."

"Do I gather that human relationships are not Sir Stafford's forte?"

"In some ways he seems totally unaware of them. On the other hand he seems to be rather good at manipulating people to get his own way, and since the decision went largely in Wes's favor, I bet it was presented as *his* decision alone."

"Ah. I suppose he uses the clout of his name and his experience of organizations such as the Trust in the interests of the manor, and to get his own way."

"Very much so. In great and little things. He and his wife have a flat in the house during the run-up to the full-time opening—a rather splendid flat carved out of some of the bedrooms on the first floor. And since he runs this festival of music and the arts almost single-handed, he has plenty of clout and patronage at his disposal."

"And he'd managed to get half the board on his side," said Felicity.

"Exactly. On the other hand, he didn't have the sense to see that getting rid of two directors in quick succession would certainly have resulted in some very bad publicity."

"I suppose the country gentry in the past could rely on discretion in the media, provided they kept their flies buttoned up."

"Even if they didn't. Money talks in a country area. But I've never heard that Stafford has problems in that direction. Or Graham either, come to that."

"The composer?"

"Yes. Stafford's brother. Much loved in the locality

I believe, when he was a young man. Gentle without side, that's what people in the village said about him. Not that the family was really gentry and therefore qualified to have 'side.' They just lived for a short time in the Dower House here on the property—Mum, Dad, kids. It was Timothy Quarles, a bachelor, living in the big house."

"I haven't had the pleasure . . ."

"Long dead. The last family member to live in the house was Rupert Fiennes. He was at the meeting this morning, but he keeps a low profile."

"I think I saw Graham, the composer, while you were in the meeting. Has he had a stroke?"

"Yes. He and his attendant seem to manage to communicate, but otherwise he's pretty much in a shell."

"So if we cut out sex, and if money matters are in the hands of a Trust, Sir Stafford is probably motivated by some kind of power lust: keeping the decisions for himself—and that means getting rid of the museum director?"

Maya shrugged. "Seems possible. You think of power-crazy people as Robert Maxwell types, but if that's what makes Stafford tick, then he's a lot more subtle about it."

"True. But if he's already got rid of one director . . ."

Maya's forehead creased. "I don't know if that was Sir Stafford. Tell you the truth, I hardly know anything about it. It was before I came on the board. But I think there was a petition from the staff questioning her competence."

"Her?"

"Oh, yes. Definitely female. Annabel Sowerby. I don't know what happened to her. They've only recently started to mention her again. Reports that she wrote while she was director get quoted, usually with the implication that she was on the ball—more so than Wesley Gannett. I'm pretty sure that's unfair to Wes and just part of the whispering campaign that the crowd around Sir Stafford have, I suspect, been organizing. Any mud is welcome, even if it means partial rehabilitation of the sacked Annabel. They rely on people's memories being short."

"But you could learn more about the sacking or suspension of Ms. Sowerby if you tried?"

"I should think so. Ben was on the board then, I'm pretty sure. Ben Hooley. He was a great help today. But what's your interest?"

Felicity decided she had better come clean.

"Raw material. I had my first novel published earlier this year, to what my agent called a 'chorus of muted praise.' The second is all but finished. I have to have a good nose for a subject if I'm going to go on, and I think I'm acquiring one. A nose, I mean. Walbrook Manor seems to have all the characteristics of a meaty plot."

Maya smiled, in obvious appreciation and interest. "There's a concert at Walbrook next Saturday. They have three or four a year to generate interest in the festival. There are still a few tickets going . . ."

Felicity thought. "I wonder if I could persuade Charlie to come. He's a policeman. Good at getting information. I suppose those were the performers we heard rehearsing? Charlie hates chamber music—calls it 'all that scraping.' Still, he's often the only black at things like that, and people come up and talk to him as some kind of interracial gesture. I might put the thumbscrews on him. We don't have any problem with babysitters."

"If you do come," said Maya, "it might be a good idea for you and me to keep apart."

"Why do you say that?"

"Some people might be unwilling to talk to your husband if they associate you with me. You don't want to get labeled—docketed as one of the awkward squad. Who knows—Sir Stafford will be intrigued that you are a novelist. He might try to sound you out. Even see if you might be interested in coming on the board."

"Well, I suppose that's better than geriatric gropings."

"Oh, Sir Stafford is not geriatric, or, so far as I know, a groper. . . . Would you be?"

"Interested? Well, in the abstract definitely not. I don't like bodies like that, and I don't think I function well on them. On the other hand, if there's something interesting going on . . ."

"I really do think there must be something, and that a good part of the board has sold its soul to the devil."

"Sir Stafford is a very smooth, subtle devil by the sound of it."

"Devils usually are. We mustn't jump to conclusions. There could be a quite different Satan at work. Do you really know what hurts most about the business of bringing Theo into the meeting? More than Sir Stafford making me think it was quite okay, then using it as an excuse to get me out of the meeting?"

"No. What?"

"All the women members of the board voted against me."

CHAPTER 2

Night Music

✳

The Music Room at Walbrook Manor had probably not been a music room until the idea of the Walbrook Festival had materialized a couple of years ago. What it had been was unclear: it was large, but not so large as the Drawing Room, through the outskirts of which tourists had tramped (hedged in by ropes) during open hours. Perhaps it was a lesser Drawing Room that the family had used when they were not entertaining. Perhaps it was used when they were throwing a not-too-distinguished ball—tenant farmers, clergymen, that sort of person. Then again, perhaps it had been Lady Quarles's Drawing Room at times when she and the Sir Whatsit Quarles of the time were not on speaking terms. Walbrook seemed a house made for collapsing marriages, and the Quarleses were rumored to be a family united to the world but liable to blowups in the privacy of their manor.

"Nice," said Felicity, looking around her.

"And very suitable," said Charlie. She shot him a

glance. He obviously didn't mean suitable for chamber concerts. Possibly he meant for mixing and mingling, for chatting and overhearing chat. Or then again perhaps he was sizing up its suitability for a scene-of-the-crime investigation should the need ever arise.

The chairs were arranged in blocks, fastened together as insisted upon by fire officers, but the blocks were separated by large areas between and behind each one so that mixing and shifting from group to group was easy. At the far end of the room was a dais with music stands and a grand piano, and the walls were hung with pictures of three centuries of the Quarles family as well as Dutch landscapes to alleviate the weight of so many determined chins and expressions of self-satisfaction. Felicity and Charlie studied the labels and the descriptions in large print for the partially sighted.

"'Arabella, Lady Quarles,'" Felicity read out. "'By Allan Ramsay.'"

"Wife of Sir Richard," put in Charlie. "Ran off with the second footman in 1764."

Felicity looked at him. "You're making it up. It doesn't say that here."

"It does on the Internet. I've done my homework."

"Hmmm. Ramsay was said to be 'born to paint women.'"

"The footman seems to have been born to provide other services. Still, she didn't have to run away with him. There must have been excellent opportunities in-house."

"What happened to her?"

"She was dead within a year, from mistreatment.

Nobody did anything to help her because she was thought to have betrayed her class."

The room was beginning to fill up. Felicity saw Maya Tyndale arrive without baby or husband, but the two let no flicker of recognition pass between them. People were not taking seats but were standing around in groups—talking, gazing at pictures, or looking a bit forlorn with the free program fluttering in their hands. Felicity was beginning to wonder if they should go up and introduce themselves to somebody when someone she recognized steamed in from a side door beside the dais, accompanied by a svelte, well-preserved woman with an air altogether more determined and businesslike than her husband's. The husband was the man Felicity had seen walking from the house to the stables the previous Saturday.

"Sir Stafford and Lady Quarles, I presume," said Felicity. "The chairman of the Walbrook Trust Board."

"Watch him," said a voice at her left arm. "Watch both of them. They'll do the room—all the new people and all the people that matter. They have it down to a fine art."

"Is he a member of the old ruling family of Walbrook?" Charlie asked.

"Yes," said the man, "but in a fairly minor way: the 'sir'-dom was for services to heritage studies." This stocky man had gray starting in his hair and a bonhomous manner. He had clearly not thought it necessary to dress up for the occasion. "I'm Ben Hooley, by the way. I'm on the Walbrook Manor Trust Board."

"I'm Felicity Peace. My husband, Charlie."

"Whoops. You must be either new or important. The old rogue is making a beeline for you."

Ben Hooley evaporated into the crowd the moment Sir Stafford arrived, his hand outstretched.

"Ahh . . . welcome to Walbrook. I haven't seen you before, have I, at Walbrook? I'm Stafford Quarles. Chairman of the Trust Board which runs the place."

"I'm Felicity Peace. This is my husband, Charlie. He's a police inspector based in Leeds. I'm a novelist—just become a real one instead of a would-be one, and the feeling is very good."

Sir Stafford's smile became more genuine. "Oh, congratulations! What a wonderful feeling of satisfaction you must get, actually holding a printed book of your own words in your hands."

Felicity was getting used to standard responses of this sort and just smiled and murmured. Why did she get the impression that Sir Stafford was more interested in the information she had just given him about Charlie's profession than in her own credentials?

"We've had an idea about grafting onto the usual musical components of the festival—the Walbrook Festival, we couldn't think of a better name—a literary element as well. Perhaps add a literary person to our board. Edinburgh has combined music and literature most successfully, and Buxton. Something like a panel of new Northern novelists, including perhaps yourself. Do you think some such thing might be a starter?"

He was so "conditional tense" that Felicity wasn't going to put money on it.

"Quite possibly. I'm only Yorkshire by adoption, not

birth, so I don't think in regional terms as a rule. Maybe my agent could help, or the Society of Authors."

"And what part do you play in this literary power-house?" Sir Stafford said, turning to Charlie, with only the slightest bit of defensiveness in his manner—something Charlie and all policemen were accustomed to.

"Oh, as sounding board, litmus paper, what you will. Felicity only reads things to me if she is quite sure it is not something I would leap on for legal reasons, or because I'd recognize the characters and tell her to be careful."

"Oh, dear! Real-life characters! I must beware." Sir Stafford gave the impression he thought he was the first person to react in this way. "Well, I do hope you'll put our little festival in your diaries. And do remember we have a very active Friends group. Ah—here's Lord Warrender. I must have a word with him . . ." His voice faded as he floated off. As Lord Warrender was only a couple of feet away and had been in his line of vision all along, Sir Stafford was probably following a preordained trail.

"Platitudinous old sod, isn't he?" said Ben Hooley, slipping back to their side. "He wields a truism so that it feels like being slapped with a wet dishcloth."

"Oh, he wasn't that bad," said Felicity. "Charlie and I both have jobs that embarrass people. They don't know how to respond to us."

"I heard the bit about your being a novelist. I must have been filling my glass when you were introduced," said Hooley, turning to Charlie.

"Police inspector," said Charlie.

"Aha! Did that faze Sir Stafford?"

"Not really. Maybe he's up on police titles—realizes that an inspector is just a dogsbody to the real high-ups—superintendent and loftier still. When anybody is impressed by the word *inspector,* it usually means they read detective novels from the thirties."

"Point taken," said Hooley. "I didn't imagine Sir Stafford had anything to hide beyond a determination to keep himself in charge of everything—having ultimate control anyway. The trustees get a look in, a say in, but we never really wield any power."

"Is the woman with him Lady Quarles?" asked Felicity. "Somehow I assumed he was a bachelor or a widower."

"The 'he never married' syndrome? Do you know, I saw that phrase in the *Times* only the other day. Some things never change. But, no—that is Lady Quarles, and she supplies the tungsten in the metal. She is the thug, he is the public face—together they are formidable."

"But are there children?"

"No. Why should that matter?"

"No—of course it doesn't. I was thinking of Sir Stafford as being part of the family who owned this place."

"Distantly, as I said. His father was a distant cousin of the last Quarles owner. No, the manor was owned in recent years by the Fiennes family. The last owner, before the Trust took over five years ago, was Rupert Fiennes. He's over there. An amiable cove who doesn't say very much and is reputed to be very pleased to be relieved of the burden of Walbrook. Old soldier, married once but long ago—the marriage didn't survive the

awfully long absences of soldiers from their families—
it's a bit like policemen: the wife and children only see
the husband for a minute or two over breakfast, if then.
Oh, Lord—I'm sorry. I forgot. Please forgive—ah, here
come the welcoming words and the music."

One of the attendants had been bustling the guests
into a loose crowd around the chairman of the Trust
standing in the doorway to the Music Room. He seemed
rather to enjoy his consequence. He cleared his throat,
smiled benignly, and began.

"Ladies and gentlemen, welcome to Walbrook. I'm
not going to go on at you. The program will tell you
about the music better than I can do. The house, as you
could guess by its style, was built in the reigns of William III and Queen Anne by the first of the Quarleses,
who had made his money from hotels, inns, and the
excellent beer consumed there. The family prospered
here for a century and a half, and then, like most of
the gentry, fell on bad times in the later-nineteenth,
early-twentieth centuries, with agricultural depression
and two terrible wars. This was a time when family
disagreements split the large family of the owners, and
there was a definite coolness between the two principal branches, the Quarleses and the Fienneses. I'm
happy to tell you this division was long ago healed, and
I value greatly the support of Rupert Fiennes and his
cousin Mary-Elizabeth for the Trust and their work for
the forthcoming festival. I think I've said enough. Too
much, I hear someone say. Then let's go in and listen to
some fine music—German music and English music—
united at last!"

The little crowd offered some scattered applause, and the attendants ushered them to the seats. It was all done with the utmost tact and efficiency, and the seats were not numbered and all were perfectly equal. Charlie admired the low-key competence of it all, and since he had been assured there was only about an hour of music, mere tasters of music to be heard later in the year at the festival, he sat down without feeling forebodings of boredom. The musicians who trouped onto the dais were young, enthusiastic looking, and were warmly applauded. The photocopied program listed two works, to be performed without interval, with more drinks afterward. After the second movement of the Schubert string quintet Charlie whispered to Felicity, "That was very good."

"Like a quiet argument or discussion," she agreed.

"Yes. Or a crime investigation."

His words suggested his immersion in the piece had not stopped him from observing both musicians and audience. He had particularly observed Sir Stafford, seated beside his lady wife, she ramrod straight of back, he smiling gently and quizzically at the young musicians. If Charlie had turned his head only slightly, he could have seen something that no doubt he was aware of: that Sir Stafford's brother had joined the audience. By the door a wheelchair had been parked, and in it was the elderly man that Felicity had already told him about: the lopsided face, the side with no motion or life in it. Beside the chair, with her back to the wall, was seated a young, competent-looking woman, obviously the attendant. The man was, Charlie knew, Graham

Quarles, the composer, who had gone in and out of fashion in his composing life, until it was cut short by, presumably, a stroke. Or was he still able to compose, dictating to some kind of musical amanuensis? Not inconceivable.

The second and last item on the program was signaled by the disappearance of the string quintet, bowing and smiling, and after some minutes, their reappearance with two wind players and three others—two singers and their accompanist. The younger singer, and the fresher of face, came a few steps forward.

"We're going to sing now—Gavin and me, with Jake accompanying—a newly found work, recently discovered among the house's archives. We'll probably know more about the cycle by the time we sing it at the festival, so I'll just introduce each song with the name of the poet and the name of the composer. Because what we have here is something rather unusual: a song cycle based on seven or eight poems from the First World War, each song the work of a different composer. The first song is called 'Rendezvous'—the poem is by Alan Seeger, killed in 1916. The song was composed by Ralph Vaughan Williams."

The young man cleared his throat and began, "'I have a rendezvous with Death . . .'"

The setting was competent but not memorable—certainly not comparable to Vaughan Williams's *On Wenlock Edge* cycle. Maybe he was not putting his heart into it.

"The second song," said the overcheerful young man, "is for baritone and will be sung by Gavin. The poem, by Isaac Rosenberg, is called 'Break of Day in the Trenches,' and it was set by Arthur Somervell."

The song was atmospheric, but stayed just short of being memorable.

"Gavin will also sing the next song, which is by a well-known person but a little-known poet. It's called 'Many a Time.' It is by a name many of you will know—Clement Attlee, onetime prime minister—and it ends with a politician's flattery of his constituents. The music is by Michael Tippett."

The music was fresh sounding, and the poem, about the isles of Greece, ended:

> *How willingly all these I would exchange*
> *To see the buses throng by Mile End Gate*
> *And smell the fried fish shops down Limehouse way.*

True politician, agreed Charlie with the young man: never takes his mind off the voters.

And so it went on, poems by Edward Thomas, Siegfried Sassoon, with music by Gurney and Bliss.

Then, coming to a fine conclusion, there was the tenor, whose name was Jamie, with Rupert Brooke on "Peace," with music by the young Britten, and splendidly, Gavin showing off his full capacity, singing Wilfred Owen's "Apologia Pro Poemate Meo"—the poem where he sees God through the mud. The music was by Peter Warlock.

Not all the audience reacted in one way, and those who were most enthusiastic also gave signs of being drained. However, there was a surprise addition to the program: Jamie then, as if emboldened by the warm applause, came forward and announced that work on the cycle was still ongoing, and that there was one song, by Ivor Gurney to words of Edward Thomas, that he would love to sing. It was probably intended to substitute for the work of Rupert Brooke—or perhaps simply be added to the corpus of the poems. He hoped people would come up and tell him their views on the poems and on the "optimum" (he liked such words) length of the cycle. He would also like comments on the title of the song cycle, currently provisionally known as *From the Trenches*. Could it be improved on? He nodded to the accompanist, sang the song called "Lights Out," then with a gesture dismissed the audience and sent them in the direction of the restocked bar.

Charlie left Felicity by the door and went and procured (at pretty outrageous prices) a glass of Chardonnay and half of a rather powerful but wholly delectable lager. When he got back to Felicity, she was talking to an elderly man.

"Oh, here is Charlie. Charlie, this is Rupert—oh, should that be *Sir* Rupert?"

"No," said the soft-spoken and courteous elderly man. "My father got a knighthood, and people sometimes assume it was hereditary, which of course it wasn't and never could be."

"Rupert Fiennes, then, this is my husband, Inspector Peace."

"Ah, Inspector—but you're not here on official matters, I assume?"

"Not at all. Felicity should have shut up about my job. I'm here as a civilian. People call me Charlie."

"Good," said Rupert. "Because we've got through all the stages of establishing the Trust so far without falling foul of the law, and we'll hope to go on that way."

"Was letting the house go painful?"

Rupert smiled broadly. "No. That's what everybody asks me. It was painful for my cousin Mary-Elizabeth, who lived here with me, but not for me."

"How long had it been in your family?"

"Since just before the war. The '39–45 war, not the one we've just been hearing about. We only moved in in 1947."

"Was it commandeered by the government for a hospital or something?"

"More or less. Mental hospital as a matter of fact. Actually I've wondered if that was how we acquired the music we've just been listening to."

"Oh, why should it be?"

"Lots of creative young people—men—were more or less destroyed mentally by the '14–'18 war. Poets, composers—you know the sort of people—driven mad by trench warfare. Now I'm fond of music, but only in a slovenly, mindless way: I like hearing music in the background, though everyone seems to complain about that. But I know, really, next to nothing about it. I do know, though, that there is a composer—mostly songs, from the interwar years—who spent most of his adult life in what they called then asylums. I'm not quite sure who it was."

"It rings a vague bell," said Felicity. "Was it Ivor

35

Gurney, the composer we've just heard? Or maybe Peter Warlock?"

"Very possibly. They're just names to me, and hardly that. I wondered whether this was a project of whoever-it-was. I'm not saying anything to any of those involved in the festival. Probably just reveal my ignorance—they'll have thought of it long ago. I'm on the board of the Trust, but I don't have to give my limitations away every time I open my mouth."

Felicity nodded, but her eyes lit up when she saw, threading his way through the crush of people, Jamie, who had introduced the song cycle. And he seemed to be coming their way.

"Excuse me," she said, catching him by the arm. If he was not aiming at their little group, he seemed delighted to talk to someone young and attractive. They were very thin on the ground. "When this place was used as a mental hospital, was Ivor Gurney ever a patient here?"

Jamie shook his head. "Oh, no. You see, he died in 1937. It seems likely that he was involved in the song cycle though. It would have seemed appropriate, I feel."

"Yes, it would. But how could he have been?"

"I'm getting vibes. Which means I'm clutching at straws blown past in the wind. Here's my provisional explanation, by which I mean guesswork. I suspect he had some hand in the whole idea of different poetic reactions to the slaughter, maybe with himself coordinating the whole scheme. It was to be a timely warning, with another war in the offing. Then he died, but by that time he'd handed on all the stuff to someone else—someone in his then home, wherever it was. When the government took over this place, this successor was moved here and brought all the papers with him. Why nothing was done about the whole idea, which was so near completion, I could make a guess at: revelations about the sheer hell of World War One didn't sit easy with the people who were prosecuting World War Two. It wouldn't have contributed to redoubling everyone's war effort, which was top of the agenda."

"That sounds very convincing."

"Yes, doesn't it?" said Jamie with a cherubic smile. "But it is just a guess. Remember that. Oh, God—there's Lord something-or-other. He's a possible sponsor. I must go and say nice things to him. As Disraeli nearly said, 'Everyone likes flattery, but when it comes to sponsors, you must lay it on with a trowel.'"

Jamie raised his hand in farewell and had only just moved away when his place was taken by somebody else, who had clearly been waiting. How could she not have noticed the woman? Felicity thought, a broad-brimmed, bellicose-breasted woman crusader, probably in her fifties and not improving with age.

"Porritt. Janet Porritt"—shoving her fist in Charlie's direction.

"Charlie Peace."

"*Inspector* Peace, eh? Or so I'm told. How did you get here?"

"My wife bought two tickets."

"No, I mean *why* are you here?"

"My wife used to teach English at the university. She's into the First World War—and of course into a lovely house like this. That's all. Policemen must have their hobbies and outside interests. People always think there must be something up when they see policemen at functions like this. It's the same with politicians. 'What's he up to?' they say. *Nothing* is the answer, in this case anyway. I'm with my wife."

"So this is your wife. I see." It sounded as if Mrs. Porritt could have said more on that subject but decided against it. "Because you know we—I mean, we on the board—are very well advised legally. And *every*thing is done by the book. Gatherings of this sort to encourage sponsorship are a feature of gallery life these days, and we've done everything—"

"Please, please," said Charlie, putting up his hand as if he were on traffic duty. "Let me say it again. I'm here socially. I'm here with my wife, and I'm here to listen to music and have a drink. There is nothing more to my visit—*nothing.*"

He turned toward Rupert Fiennes, and Mrs. Porritt began to chunter, not too silently, going away.

"Sorry I'm sure," she said over her shoulder. "Only trying to help."

Felicity grinned at her husband. "You've just uttered a half-truth or two."

"Not for the first time," said Charlie cheerfully. "And some of the others have been on oath. Fancy a walk in the gardens? Get rid of the alcohol fumes, and the fumes of self-righteousness?"

"Yes—I'd like to see the gardens at night."

They moved out into the larger Drawing Room, then through to the entrance hall, where the usual admission-charge booth was situated—not manned to extract cash at this hour, but still manned, by a large, broad-shouldered man. They smiled and drifted out through the main door and then round to the side of the house that sloped down to the lodge, and the converted-stables building. The solidity of the manor hushed to a whisper the high-pitched talk of the would-be or could-be patrons, and for a moment there was silence, broken almost immediately by a voice.

"Doesn't it seem the most peaceful place on earth?"

Turning, they saw the man they had just passed in the hall. They had taken him for a bouncer, or for a more genteel equivalent of one. Perhaps they had been mistaken.

"Hello. I'm Felicity Peace. Do I detect an Australian accent?"

The man grimaced. "Just a trace. A bloody soupçon. I have noticed it prevents a lot of people in this country from taking me seriously. So I've decreased the Shane Warne touches."

"You shouldn't take it too seriously. The same people as flinch at yours would also flinch at a Birmingham accent, or an Ulster one. They're not to be taken seriously. This is my husband, Charlie."

"And one who's also had trouble here with his accent—in my case Cockney."

"Hello," said the man, shaking his hand. "Welcome to Walbrook. I know you're a policeman, and that's why I followed you." His glance strayed to the path from the house that came from the other side of it, but also led down to the stables. Sir Stafford and Lady Quarles were walking slowly, with a sort of stateliness, hand in hand. They stopped a couple of hundred yards away and looked round the magnificent vista. "It struck me," the man went on, "that we have a lot of contacts with lawyers, but we have none at all with policemen. I'm Wes Gannett, the director here. Graduate of the University of Sydney. I wondered if we three could get to know each other, just so that when I need a bit of advice—or even, perhaps, you, Inspector, needed a bit of information or background stuff to an art robbery or something of that sort—we might contact each other."

Charlie thought. "You know there is some vague talk of co-opting Felicity onto the board of the Trust?"

"Oh, good."

"That doesn't bother you?"

"Not at all. The Trust is—how shall we put it?—a variegated body. I'd like to add a member who does not think me a ruffian who is two generations away from the convicts and thus unfitted to take care of one of England's minor heritage buildings."

"I see. Well, I've no objections to staying in touch on matters of mutual interest."

"That's great," said Wes, apparently sincerely glad and grateful. "My wife died last year. It was a blow to me in every way. I don't do cooking, but there is a fine cook in the village who's already volunteered her services when I want to entertain. Perhaps you could come round and the three of us could have an unstructured discussion over dinner?"

"Delighted to," said Felicity. Her eyes strayed to Sir Stafford and Lady Quarles. "They look so peacefully happy. From a distance."

"So, I'm sure, did Burke and Hare," said Charlie.

"And in love," said Felicity, ignoring him.

"My knowledge of Burke and Hare doesn't extend that far."

"They certainly seem contented," said Wes Gannett. "They've got everything they wanted."

Felicity digested this.

"Have you ever wondered," she asked, "why you were given the job here?"

"Yes."

"Because with your Australian background you were surely less experienced in the necessary fields than some of the British applicants—and there must have been many of them. And your one or two stately homes in Australia would be very different."

"Oh, very different. In any case I've not been employed in any of them."

"So why do you think you got the position?"

A little smile played around Wes's full lips. "Perhaps for the very reasons you've just mentioned as making me an unlikely appointee."

"'Where ignorance is bliss—'"

"They'd be unwise to rely too much on my ignorance," said Wes Gannett.

CHAPTER 3

Reconnaissance

✳

The letter to Felicity was not slow in coming—less than a week after the concert at Walbrook Manor it arrived, on thick notepaper resistant to the hands. "Dear Mrs. Peace," Sir Stafford's letter began. How did he decide how to address me? Felicity wondered. Not Miss Coggenhoe, her maiden name, which he probably didn't know. Not Ms. Peace or Ms. Coggenhoe. She thought, I suppose I'm showing I've passed my sell-by date just for thinking about it.

I have consulted with all the members of the Walbrook Manor Trust Board, and by a big majority they were in favor of your being offered a place on the Trust Board. I am delighted. Your own achievements in fiction, your position as a part-time lecturer at Leeds University, with some degree of specialization in early-twentieth-century literature, and above all your obvious lively interest in all the arts, which is so desirable for a Trust which will have responsibilities that span a wide spectrum, make you a clear choice for the position.

You will be very welcome, and I look forward to introducing you to your fellow trustees at a meeting on Saturday, January 14th, in Walbrook's stable complex.

> Yours sincerely,
> Stafford

Felicity thought this over for a couple of days so as not to be thought to be too enthusiastic, then replied:

Dear Sir Stafford,

I was pleased and honored that you and the Board of Trustees thought I might be useful to the Walbrook Trust. I am happy to accept and look forward to an enjoyable and useful period on the board. Perhaps I should tour Walbrook before the first meeting to see how it will be organized before Spring, when the more extensive opening times will become operative. This will be a very exciting time for the Trust—especially so for you, and now for me too.

> Yours sincerely,
> Felicity Peace

That letter produced a response. Sir Stafford wrote back immediately to say he was pleased that she could accept his offer, that if she would tell him when she would come, he would do his best to be available and would show her the behind-the-scenes aspects of the operation. If he was occupied elsewhere, "I will ask my wife to do the honors of the dear old house, which she and I both love so much."

Felicity noted the cool tone of the letters. She had the feeling that Sir Stafford and Lady Quarles were already taking on the mantle of lord and lady of the manor. She decided that, before visiting Walbrook for a guided tour (which was what she would undoubtedly be given whatever she might actually prefer), she would visit on a Tuesday and see as much as was possible to see *by herself.* She always set great store on her own observation and felt it was necessary to see the place on her own before a hurried tour that tried to put ideas into her mind. Therefore shortly before Christmas she put Thomas into his occasional nursemaid's care and drove to Walbrook for what she hoped would be a leisurely tour, ready to explain why she needed to come early and unannounced to take her own view of the house and its visitors.

"Hello," she said at the admissions desk. "I'm—"

"Oh, I saw you at the concert," said the middle-aged woman behind the grill. "You're coming on the board, aren't you? You're very welcome, Mrs. Peace—"

"Felicity."

"Ah—Sir Stafford was not quite sure." The woman put her hand up to her mouth. "Forgets things he's just been told and makes a lot of mistakes. Nothing too terrible as yet, so we live in hope . . ."

"It will come to us all," said Felicity comfortably. "My husband calls it 'the great unmentionable topic.'"

"He has a point. Now, you must accept a free ticket today, as a gesture—"

"Do you mind if I don't? I'd like to start as I mean to go on. I'll pay the normal entrance fee."

"Very well, if you prefer." The attendant was bridling a little at the rejection of her gesture. "It's six pounds. . . . Thank you very much. You're very generous."

"Not at all," said Felicity as she turned and walked into the first room of the house. As she began the tour in the manner and direction that pasted-up notices suggested, she heard the telephone being taken up in the attendant's booth.

She took in first the Long Drawing Room, which she had seen the night of the concert. Ropes hindered her tour, stretching from the hall door to the one into the next downstairs room, and they thus kept her from a close scrutiny of the furniture, which looked in less than pristine condition, and of the fine mantelpiece, rather overdressed with vases and small statues. The pictures too were not to be inspected too closely. There was provided, however, one of those little table-tennis bats to inform the visitor about the most important pictures—in this case portraits by the ubiquitous Allan Ramsay, with a small Reynolds of three young children, a Gainsborough, and to vary the monotony of similar-shaped and expressionless faces, a seascape by Constable. Felicity guessed that the bigger names were not represented by examples of their better works.

She passed into the next room.

This was what had been described on her last visit to

the house as the Music Room, where the concert had taken place. It was still described in the same way on a neat, little placard over the door. As she walked through, the attendant who had watched her tour round the Long Drawing Room slipped through and watched her in the smaller one. Felicity took in the whole room and one change immediately struck her.

"The picture over there," she said to the woman. "I was here for the concert ten days ago, and there was a picture of a rather luscious eighteenth-century lady. It's gone, and now we have a very respectable Victorian lady."

"Oh, yes. They came and made the changeover last week, before opening time. It's not *going*. It had been away for cleaning and restoration, and it was hurried up so it could be in place for the concert. Now Sir Stafford is going to inspect it to see if the restorers have done all we asked them to do."

"Oh, I see. I suppose she's popular with visitors."

"Well, she was very pretty, wasn't she? And I believe the person who painted it was well known, though I can't now remember his name."

"Yes. . . . And of course that particular Lady Quarles ran off with the footman, which gives it a definite interest of a kind."

"Oh, it does." The woman leaned forward to confide something usually kept secret. "Only we don't volunteer that sort of information—it seems . . . inappropriate." She was obviously using a word that had been fed to her.

"Does it?" said Felicity. "It's a very long time ago."

"Oh, but we're sort of custodians. We have to think of the feelings of the family who used to live here."

"I suppose you do, even if they're mostly dead. What was the family called? Or was there more than one family who was called 'Lord of the Manor'?"

"I believe there was. There were the Fienneses—it was one of them who gave the manor over to the Trust. He's a lovely old boy—one of the real old-fashioned gentlemen—you know the type. You don't meet them often these days." The woman was procrastinating, Felicity felt sure, because his was the only name she knew.

"I heard they were fairly recent, the Fienneses."

"Yes, I believe so. About the time of the war—I'm not sure which one."

"The picture was of a Lady Arabella Quarles." I'm feeding her, Felicity thought.

"Quarles! That's it! Sir Stafford's branch. I'll forget my own name next. The Quarleses got into financial difficulties and the Fienneses bought the manor from them. They didn't last long though. You need a bottomless purse these days to own a house and an estate like this one."

"I'm sure you do. Thank you so much for the information."

Felicity suspected she heard a sigh of relief when she moved on. At least there was no danger of visitors being caught in an endless spiel by the volunteer museum assistant who wants to tell everything he or she knows. The limits of her information would quickly be reached with Marcia Phelps, the name Felicity had learned from the lady's lapel badge.

The direction placards, dominated by large arrows, took Felicity via a short corridor to the Estate's Office. Here the administration was centered, led by whoever—family or employee—was in charge. She began by looking at photographs and letters that aimed to show Walbrook in its social context, and she decided the custodial work had been successful: the manor was shown as part of rural life in West Yorkshire—the house's family mingling at shows and race meetings in the most amiable of styles. Felicity, though, could not rid herself of the feeling that the house, centered on those rolling lawns, with an entry gate about half a mile away, was essentially solitary, and the family likewise.

"I hope you find the display interesting."

The voice came from the door.

"Very much so, Lady Quarles." Felicity spoke without looking up, then tore her eyes from the photographs of a prize bull and its owner and smiled.

"You recognized my voice. How flattering. When they told me you were here, I came down because there's no guarantee we won't both—Stafford and I— be engaged when you come next Tuesday." That put Felicity in her place as far as matters of importance were concerned. "You've seen the two drawing rooms, already, haven't you? If we could just do the other rooms, I'll rest happy that we've done our bit. You like this room?"

"I do. Very much. The house seems a bit remote and cut off at first sight, but of course it is part of the agricultural jigsaw of the county."

"Stafford has many more photographs and he has only to choose which will go best in here. I've already had to dissuade him from choosing one of himself as a little boy, in the doorway of the Dower House."

"So Sir Stafford has a real connection with the house and the family?"

"Oh, certainly. When his mother was dangerously ill, he and his father stayed in the Dower House for more than three months, to be near to her in the Leeds Infirmary. But in spite of the Quarles name, they weren't close to the Walbrook family by birth. The old family did their duty, though not really enthusiastically: when there were relations to be entertained, they were put in the Dower House with a first basketful of groceries in the cupboard. They were asked up to the manor for dinner once a week and otherwise left alone."

"Still, that may have been wise in the circumstances—the sick wife and so on. I must go and see the Dower House, maybe next Tuesday. I expect the stay there made a big impression on Sir Stafford."

"Well, it must have. He was only three, and war was about to begin. But when the question arose as to what could be done with the manor, because poor old Rupert was determined to rid himself of the burden—"

"That was how Mr. Fiennes saw it, was it?"

"Oh, absolutely. Stafford is doing him a service. He'd been curator and director in all sorts of galleries, museums, and historic properties during his long career, and he came up with the solution of a Trust, with Walbrook at its heart—serving in fact a double function."

"What was that?"

"First as a specimen of the sort of property owned by the landed gentry of this area in the last four centuries. Second as a location for secondary, smaller exhibitions, primarily of a historical or literary nature. Stafford saw at once that there had to be a changing attraction that would bring people to Walbrook at least once a year. Our first exhibition will be the First World War and its poets, which will go on to Aberdeen after we've had it. Next year there may be one on twentieth-century children's writers. My idea, so I hope it comes off. And then perhaps one on royal consorts. Ah—here we are."

While they were talking, they had turned and walked back through the drawing rooms, into the hall where the cash register was, and then up the staircase. Lady Quarles swung round and gazed at the picture-rich stairwell. She pointed to a rather lifeless early portrait.

"The founder of the Quarles family prosperity. Sixteen thirty to 1693. Went into exile after the execution of Charles I and clung on to Charles II until the Restoration. Did very nicely afterwards, as you could imagine. He left the sort of fortune that could build a lovely house like this. Of course people commented on the will: how could a rural hotelier amass that sort of wealth unless by swindling, and so on. He ignored them, and he was planning the house and foundations when he died."

"So it was a Queen Anne house?"

"Yes, finished when she was on the throne. I doubt

if that description has any meaning beyond that she happened to be queen, and people made a great deal of money during her reign. Look at the Duke of Marlborough. Well, now, there's not a great deal to see here, though there will be. There is this landing, which is nice and spacious, and Stafford says it will be marvelous for displaying pictures."

"I can see that. Do you have a lot of pictures in reserve?"

Lady Quarles screwed up her face. "Not really. Though they employed Allan Ramsay—everybody did—the family didn't have much of an eye for artistic talent. We might be able to borrow some pictures. Alternatively if we have a larger-than-usual exhibition up here, this area could house overspill or any larger exhibit."

Lady Quarles turned and walked along part of the corridor.

"This and the other corridor will be the exhibition area, except the last three rooms of the other corridor going north, which are for the moment Stafford's and my flat. In the course of nature we won't be occupying those rooms forever, but they are quite convenient for now."

"I won't ask you to show me."

"No, don't. I'm not a housewife."

"But they come within the remit of the Trust?"

"Oh, yes, technically. The Trust is responsible for *all* the buildings on the estate, all the gardens and fields, and of course all the house."

"A rather daunting responsibility."

"Except that we have a director, who can be relied on to decide most things. And if he doesn't have the experience to solve all the problems, there are various bodies—for museums and galleries I mean—that can offer excellent advice, estimated costings, and so on. Now, I'll just show you the empty rooms. . . ."

"Please."

Lady Quarles threw open a door that did indeed show Felicity nothing but an empty room.

"This is going to be the first room of the exhibition. We plan to call it Recruitment and Conscription. It will cover how the young men were persuaded to join up, and how they were trained. The next room . . ."

She threw open another door. This time the empty room was tiny.

"This was a dressing room for the bedroom you've just seen. Women at War is the topic. How women aided the war effort by sewing uniforms in factories, ran hospitals and recuperation centers, even helped in the manufacture of armaments and ammunitions."

"The end of women as useless decorations," said Felicity.

"The beginning of the end, anyway. Did you know that even between the wars a woman teacher in the state system who got married had to resign? It was to be a long fight."

Lady Quarles sounded sincerely indignant, and Felicity liked her the better for it.

"The next room is the biggest of the bedrooms. The theme is the Life in the Trenches. It is big, but Stafford and I both felt we needed space for a really big picture—

oil painting presumably—to convey the full horror of it, of trench life. It may turn out to be too big for this room, and if it is, we shall have to spread our wings and put it on the landing. But no matter—it would probably look mightily impressive there."

"You've got something in mind?"

"Two or three possibilities. We want it to be really authentic, by someone who had experienced, or at the very least observed, the slaughter. Someone who only knew of the horror by word of mouth would probably be someone who would play down the horrific aspects—an apologist. So we, and Wes, will be investigating in so far as we can. They're very helpful at the Imperial War Museum, though they haven't themselves got anything that answers the purpose. Which speaks volumes . . ."

She led the way to the last room, almost as big as the previous one.

"Then comes the Approach of Peace. This means the last year, the last Allied push, and the German surrender."

"Will you take that into the aftermath—all the young men with severe mental problems and so on?"

"If we have room."

Felicity had gone over to a photograph, one of several left higgledy-piggledy on an old table.

"That's—"

"Wilfred Owen."

"Yes. I thought it might be Ivor Gurney. He had a real, though rather remote, connection with the house, didn't he?"

"Yes, but he never, so far as we know, was here. You think he ought to be highlighted, but it's Owen who everyone reads."

"As they should. It's just that—"

"I know, I know, but you know how it is. The Romantic movement is Wordsworth and Coleridge in the older generation, Byron, Shelley, and Keats in the younger. No one else—people like Southey, Leigh Hunt, or Tom Moore—gets a look in. People will remember that they saw a photo of Wilfred Owen here, will talk about it to literary folk, but if they said, 'They've got a snapshot of Ivor Gurney,' they'd be met with 'Who?' And it's partly you university folk who are to blame."

Felicity nodded. "You're quite right."

"Stafford is. He knows all there is to know about museums. Including literary museums. Now—that's really all there is, as yet. Do you have any questions?"

Felicity frowned and thought.

"One or two, nitty-gritty ones. Finance. Is the exhibition—the World War One, children's literature, whatever—separate from the main part of the house, and will visitors pay a special entry fee to see it?"

"Not finally decided. They'll make the decision at the January board meeting. Making them separate would mean more staff, volunteer or paid. I'd bet they go for one entry payment for the whole house. But of course you'll be one of the voters, part of the solution, you might say."

"And will Wes be in charge of all the exhibitions, or will you take some visiting exhibitions that have been curated elsewhere?"

"After this first one the door is open for very good exhibitions of the right size or any that we could cut down to size or add to, to make them right. But I don't imagine that will happen very often. There is only one exhibition a year, after all, and Wes will want to make his mark—quite right too."

"Yes, I imagine he will. Thank you so much for showing me round," said Felicity. "If I really am part of the solution, I'm a much better informed part now."

They shook hands, and Felicity went down the magnificent staircase, which would show off pictures so well, then past the entry point and out into pale winter sunlight. As she walked, she realized she had seen nothing of the behind-the-scenes Walbrook that she had been promised.

Felicity had a couple of hours before she needed to collect Thomas. She was irresistibly drawn to the spacious grounds, to see them once more with her now-better-informed mind. She could see that developers must have viewed these spacious fields and gardens with a greedy eye. Whether the house was demolished or not, the property represented potential profit. The house could be divided into flats, the fields covered with prestigious mini-mansions for bankers, accountants, estate managers. The mass-market builders must send up imprecations every Sunday to bring about the downfall or death of Sir Stafford, or whoever had thought up the Trust solution.

She wondered who that was. Was it Sir Stafford, as his wife had said? More likely Rupert Fiennes. The Trust got the property off his shoulders without giving him a guilt complex about betraying the place to commercial exploitation or to a family of newcomers. She had realized during the tour around the house and exhibition that the Quarles family were the traditional, long-standing owners of the house, and Rupert was only one of the interlopers who had taken over in the forties. How were the Fienneses related to the Quarleses? she wondered. She'd have to hunt Rupert out and have a chat.

CHAPTER 4

Entertaining

✳

When Wes Gannett had finished the arrangement of his dining room, he stood in the doorway to look at the results of his labors. There were not many results, and there had not been much labor. Would Felicity Peace approve? People react strongly against overpreparation, Wes's wife had often said. They feel they've been put in a stage set, like Violetta in act 1 of *Traviata*, in a much too swish and tasteful decor. The room should look much as it did every day, then the guest could relax into comfort and welcome. As so often, his wife had been right. Hardly an hour went by in which Wes did not think of her.

Felicity arrived about twenty past seven, sank into an armchair, and said an exhausted "Yes" to gin and tonic.

"Charlie *may* be here about a quarter to eight," she said. "That's if nothing comes up at the end of his shift, which it very often does. He says to start eating when you intended to and make no concessions to the conditions of his rotten job."

"I think I'd like your husband's wry sense of humor," said Wes, coming over with two glasses. "We share job dissatisfaction too."

"I quite like his humor myself, normally," said Felicity, "but it makes him accept without protest some pretty archaic working practices."

"Shall we wait the talk for him, if not the food?"

"No, no. I'll fill him in on any vital info. How shall we do it? Question and answer?"

"If that seems to you a good idea."

"One thing I'd like you to tell me about," she said, sucking her slice of lemon, "is the family—the Quarleses and the Fienneses. I found I knew more than your unpaid attendant when I went round the other week, but still I know pathetically little."

Wes nodded. "Join the club. I'm preparing a ten- or twelve-page booklet—not for sale in the shop, but for the attendants, when they're asked questions, if they deign to read it. So I am a step or two ahead of you, though in the two years I've been here it has mostly been a fug. What do you want to know?"

"The relationship between the two branches of the family, and how the house came to slide from one branch to the other."

"That's rather good," said Wes appreciatively. "I might nick it for the pamphlet, if you don't mind. That's called making you pay for your dinner."

"You're welcome. Now, go right back to William and Mary, or James the Second or whoever is relevant to the family history."

"Let's start with Queen Anne. That turn-of-the-century

age was the last years of Charles James Quarles, the old villain. He had a number of hotels—we today would call it a chain—and, most importantly, the majority of them were in London. They were luxury hotels, with maids included in the room price, and everything shipshape and paid for."

"His spirit lingers on today," said Felicity.

"I've never been offered a maid," said Wes, "but, yes—you're spot-on. The family most years made handsome profits and set up as country gentry in Yorkshire, one of the cheapest counties in the country at the time. They built the house you know, and generation after generation did the sort of things the landed gentry did do."

"What exactly was that?"

"They farmed, sold and leased out land, were magistrates, one was an MP . . ."

"Distinguished?"

"Extremely so in the nineteenth century. He supported Gladstone, then took fright at his radicalism and switched to 'Disraeli and Empire.' He got elected to parliament every time, whatever he stood for. And through it all the Quarleses did very well, and they ruled and reigned."

"And were loved by the tenantry?"

"This side of idolatry, that's my impression." Wes got up and went to the sideboard, where Felicity saw a tape recorder was plugged in. "I thought you might like to hear a bit of this. I've been talking to people, particularly old people, about the house and the family—for the pamphlet and to add to the archive. This is Jeb Wheeler, a ninety-year-old, and 'a right cantankerous old bugger,' as one of the museum assistants called him. I asked him a question about how the Quarles family was viewed in the West Riding as it was then called in Yorkshire."

Wes switched on the machine.

"Well, of course they were highly respected," came the old but clear and opinionated voice. "Very highly respected. That's what we said to reporters if the family ever got into the news, and to tourists, hikers, students, and the like. Of course they were highly respected. They owned most of the farms, they could get you sacked for the littlest thing—behind with the rent, a nice bit of cheek when you were in your cups, your daughter scoring with the heir to the estates. The family had all the big cards you see."

"And did they use them?" came Wes Gannett's voice.

"Oh, aye, they used them," said the hectoring old voice. "And quite cunning they were too. They did it, and never did it so as to lose the support of what folk nowadays call the middle classes. Professional people— doctors, solicitors, clergy, schoolteachers—oh, they were Fortune's darlings till the twentieth century came and cut them down to size."

Wes leaned over and switched the recorder off.

"Oh, I wanted to hear how they were cut down," protested Felicity.

"So did I, but I never got anything concrete from him. I concluded that he wasn't just clamming up, he didn't really understand what had happened, only that something *had* happened, not just to the Quarleses, but to all their class."

"Couldn't you find out from these 'professional people' that he sneers at?"

"I got scraps from them—usually from just letting them talk. Press them and they go shtum—still: old instincts reasserting themselves. Things had been getting tough in the last decades of the nineteenth century. Lady Bracknell in *The Importance of Being Earnest* says something about 'land has ceased to be either a profit or a pleasure,' and that was the root of the family's problems. Then there was the First World War, which killed off the eldest son of the Quarleses. Doubly unfortunate because the second son was a bit of an ass—went in for all sorts of madcap schemes, was fooled by dodgy investments. I don't know the details, but just before the Second World War the crunch came and they had to sell the house to a member of the junior branch of the family—the Fiennes. I couldn't pinpoint the problems, but after the house was requisitioned for a mental hospital during the war, the Fiennes took it back under their control in 1947, but they never really made a go of it."

"Hence Rupert and his desire to be rid of it."

"Exactly. By the way, I rather guess he's the best of the family, and by far."

Felicity smiled. "I confess I liked what I saw, and heard, of him."

"And that wasn't true of Sir Stafford, I'd guess."

"Reserve judgment. My first board meeting is still to come, and I can't readily pass judgment, especially as I've heard derogatory opinions of him recently from a member of the board. What exactly was wrong with

Rupert's branch of the family? Why couldn't they make the house and the family business pay?"

"Lack of strong business sense I'd guess. Rupert's father had it, but Rupert didn't. It happened to a lot of the gentry families in this country," said Wes. "Even in the times when agriculture was paying—or the European Union was paying—hand over fist and rural farmers had whopping great cars and sent their children to snooty schools, that didn't last, and if they hadn't stashed away a good part of their gains, they just dipped down in the social scale and spent their time wondering where the next check was coming from."

"I feel rather glad Rupert lacks business instincts," said Felicity.

"There's no way I could argue with that. Though Mary-Elizabeth has a sharp little eye—natural, not trained, and it's been useful now and then. I'm going to need all my instincts to get the Trust running and make the house a success."

"What was Rupert before he took over the running of the house?"

"An undistinguished but honorable career in the army."

"Oh. That surprises me a little."

"I think he discovered he was not the type to prosper in that organization. People whisper that he was disillusioned by the Falklands War in the 1980s. Thought it was mishandled from the start. Thinks the Thatcher government sent all the wrong signals to the Argentine government."

"Rather a brave man, then."

"Criticizing the Thatcher government in this part of the country? Yes, rather. Especially as his family was the sort that would naturally be among her supporters. . . . Ah, the bell!"

The buzz had come from the kitchen. As she took her place at the table, Felicity caught sight of a mousy-looking woman taking plates out of the oven.

"I'll tell cook to keep a plateful hot for your husband," said Wes, grinning wryly at how country gentry he sounded. He was just pushing his chair back when there came a ring at the front door, which Wes answered, coming back with a Charlie who was clearly frozen, rubbing his hands and pulling from around his ear what looked like a balaclava helmet.

"Oh, Australian warmth," he said, looking around appreciatively, "never was it more welcome. I had a lift from Hargreaves in the chilliest police car I've ever known. Looks as if I've come at the right time too."

Wes ushered him to a chair. "I act as waitress at meals, to assuage my conscience about employing paid labor. Sit down, Charlie—nourishment is on its way, and I'll only be a minute or two. Felicity can bring you up to speed with what we've been talking about."

Which she did in suitably digest form, finishing up when Wes came in bearing a tray full of plates, which all held mushroom risotto.

"All right, Charlie? Get the main points?"

"I think so. I have to keep telling myself that what we're pondering is not a crime, just a situation. What does the situation consist of? First of all, two attempts, one of them successful, to get rid of the directors. Note, the director is the employee most concerned with and knowledgeable about museums—the running of them, the aspects of conservation, provenance, authenticity, and so on. Successful dismissal in the case of the first director . . . Name?"

"Annabel Sowerby."

"Annabel Sowerby. Edged out, I believe. Reason given, in the utmost confidence, that she wasn't up to the job. Her going, we may say, saved you, Mr. Gannett—"

"Wes, if you can bear it. I see some English people flinch at it."

"Wes it is. All sorts of questions arise, mostly connected with Sir Stafford, who seems to have taken the lead in trying to give the boot to the two of you, unsuccessful in your case. Questions, as I say, arise: Why does Sir Stafford, the man most knowledgeable and experienced in museum management, want to get rid of the one person who rivals him in those qualities? Why didn't he think of the inevitable bad publicity if he'd succeeded with you? What baggage is carried by Sir Stafford concerning Walbrook Manor—is there anything more than the rather frail connection of his living in the Dower House as a child with a dying mother? Is Lady Quarles connected in any way with Walbrook, other than by marriage? I could go on."

Wes Gannett nodded. "Your questions really provide a sort of summing up of puzzling aspects of the present situation. What about standing back from that, and from Sir Stafford, and pinpointing the larger picture?"

Charlie shifted in his seat. "Again, the danger is my

being a policeman. As such I'd like to know what the last of the Quarleses did with his money. He was so unwise that he was forced to call in a distant relative, Rupert Fiennes's father, to whom he sold the whole caboodle. Questions abound in my mind, and since this is a factual matter, we ought to be able to come up with some answers."

"We mustn't forget your tape recording of your oldest inhabitant, who took a dim view of both branches of the family, I'd guess," said Felicity to Wes.

"Yes. An entertaining fellow, but it would be better to find someone without the bias. A local historian for example."

"Maybe," said Charlie. "Though it seems likely that the transfer of the house was mainly a family matter, and it could have been kept within the family."

"There'd be sure to be gossip," said Felicity.

"Exactly. And gossip, though often misleading, has been known to be right. What about starting with Mr. Rupert Fiennes, and if he's uncooperative, try to find either other old residents or people whose parents had strong connections with the manor—the butler's illicit offspring, for example."

"Butler?" said Wes. "Not by the 1930s I'd guess. Eighteen ninety maybe, but by the thirties a butler would be a thing of the past at Walbrook."

"Point taken. Another interesting development: Sir Stafford and his lady wife have taken over rooms in the manor to serve as a flat for themselves. One can see the need for that while the status and routine of the house is being established, but do they have wider ambitions—to be accepted in the area as the lord and lady of Walbrook? A fairly innocent piece of vanity, but they are occupying rooms that could better be used for the exhibitions that are going to be part of Walbook's appeal."

"Yes. I can't at the moment see the relevance of that, but it's interesting that another member of the Quarles wing of the family is already in residence," said Charlie, looking around him.

"The composer," said Felicity. "Graham Quarles."

"Yes," said Charlie. "And if he is not party to any silly plot or plan on Sir Stafford's part, and if Rupert Fiennes doesn't hand out the dirt on his branch of the family, perhaps we could get our missing information from Graham."

"He is severely handicapped," said Felicity. "But that may not have affected his memory."

"Before we go on," said Charlie, "I was talking the other day to the chief constable about trustees and charities and suchlike, and there are questions nowadays about the many eminent or vaguely well-known people, often of the aristocracy, who get put on the many governing bodies of charities. Often they get their names on the society's letterhead and so on, and then use that for their own purposes. Rent-free accommodation is frequently a perk when in fact the job is merely nominal or ornamental, and no work demanding their presence at the charity's headquarters is ever done."

"Interesting," said Felicity.

"He also said that the people who get put on these bodies' governing councils are often quite innocent of any knowledge of museums, galleries, or whatever the body caters for. He says they not infrequently get inferiority complexes about their lack of knowledge compared to the professional employee and try their damnedest to get rid of them."

They thought about this.

"But *innocent* hardly applies to Sir Stafford," said Felicity. "He's spent most of his life around galleries and museums and is very knowledgeable."

"But you weren't thinking of Sir Stafford, were you?" said Wes, turning to Charlie.

"No," said Charlie. "I was thinking of the people he's chosen to go on the board of the Walbrook Trust. He'll have looked for people he thinks he can manipulate."

"He's looking for people with a combination of qualities," said Wes. "Easy to manipulate but also ignorant of stately home museums. In me he's got the second quality maybe, particularly of English museums. But he hasn't got the first."

"And he'll get a surprise with Felicity," said Charlie in heartfelt tones. "But can we turn to a related subject which you could help us with, Wes?" The director was just handing to him a plate of sticky toffee pudding. Charlie licked his lips and tucked in. "The concert I came to, Wes. It had a Schubert piece, then a newly discovered work which was a sort of collaborative effort. Well-known composers and not-so-well-known ones putting together a—what do you call it?—a song cycle, based on poems from the First World War."

"And mostly written by men who actually fought in the war," said Wes.

"Yes. Now the implication seemed to float in the air

that there was a connection between this collaboration—or perhaps between just two or three of the composers—and Walbrook Manor. But in fact no connection was spelled out, and it's difficult to see that it could be. Do you know?"

Wes shifted from buttock to buttock. "Well-spotted, Charlie, but I have little to offer. For a start, the festival, where the premiere of the piece will take place, does not come within my remit. It's entirely under the control of the cultural subcommittee on the board. So there was no reason why I should be told anything, and since that's the case, I was *not* told anything. Sir Stafford saw to that."

"Didn't you ask?"

"Oh, sure, I asked. I was told the new song was found in drawers in the bedroom of their flat."

"Sir Stafford and his wife's? The rooms they have taken over as their place of residence?" asked Felicity.

"The very place. Weren't you taken there when you visited? Lady Quarles told me she had given you a tour."

"I was not. Lady Quarles said she was no housewife and the place was in a mess."

"Personally," said Wes Gannett as if addressing Parliament, "I regard Lady Quarles as a model of orderliness. I would guess that the flat reflects that—perpetually in order so the queen could pay a visit if she chose."

"Take for granted that there *is* a connection of the song cycle with Walbrook," said Charlie, "then the connection would most likely be in the thirties, when the prospect of another war led people to look back to the war of '14–'18 as a dreadful warning. That would rule out any connection with Graham Quarles. He would have been either unborn or too young."

"But is there any other connection between Walbrook and music?" asked Felicity. "Nobody has mentioned one to me."

"There's probably none," said Wes. "There's no particular connection of the house to the First World War, but it was chosen as the subject of the first exhibition because it will attract a lot of attention in schools. The festival of course is separate from the exhibition. If what the men sang in the concert is a genuine cycle, not one forged to sing to order, I'd say the most likely connection would be to the Second World War, when Walbrook was taken over for use as a mental asylum."

"Why? Is there any strong connection between music and madness?" asked Charlie.

"No more than with art, I suppose," said Wes. "But mental disturbance was one consequence of serving in the First World War, and specially in the trenches. Ivor Gurney was one of several young musicians who never really recovered."

"And was he kept in the asylum that was established here?" asked Felicity.

"No. For the good reason that he died in 1937."

"I could ask about him, and music, at the next board meeting," said Felicity.

"Good luck to you. Better luck, in fact, than I ever had."

Wes's remark must have taken root in Charlie's mind and sprouted a lot of ramifications, because on the drive home in Felicity's car, and apropos of little, Charlie said,

"I wonder why Wes didn't seem to want either of us to go and talk to that grumpy old yokel he'd taped."

"I don't know that he had any such feeling," said Felicity.

"There you are, and you a novelist too."

"What's that got to do with anything?"

"You've got to learn to listen to the voice behind the voice," said Charlie.

CHAPTER 5

Back to the Thirties

✳

Felicity, since the publication of her first novel, had advanced in status and self-confidence and had loosened her connection with the English Department at Leeds University. Frail connections there still were, however: she had the small class "Male Portraiture in Female Novelists" and she had a couple of honors students. She valued the links, liked her students, and found the teaching dimension a valuable prop. Once a fortnight she went in, to give the class on male characters and return the odd essay or thesis chapters.

One of the most valuable links was Joan Wythers, the English Department secretary. If she was not too busy, Felicity could use her to keep up to date with departmental gossip, personal or academic. A week after her dinner with Wes, and only a few days before her first board meeting of the Walbrook Trust, she was surprised to be accosted by Joan as soon as she came through the door.

"Hello, Felicity! What's this I hear about you and

Walbrook Manor? You've been keeping very quiet about it."

"I haven't been keeping quiet. I just haven't brought it up. Why should I? What's your interest? I've always thought of you as Leeds through and through."

"You're not wrong. But my family's roots are in Walbrook village. My mother was the first to move away to the Big Town."

"Why did she do that?"

"To get a job that paid more than a starvation wage. But in my childhood we were always going back there, to see the whole roster of relatives and school friends. So I think of myself, somehow, as a Walbrook person."

"Did your mother ever work there?"

"Not really—not full-time. From time to time when there was a vacancy, she went to fill in if she was asked. She didn't like the family much, but the money, such as it was, was useful."

"Wasn't your mother an unmarried parent?"

"She was, and at a time when it was a matter of scandal and tut-tut. She felt she was always being reminded of it, and that it was used to keep her wages at rock bottom."

"Who was head of the family then?"

"Do you know Rupert Fiennes?"

"Yes, a little."

"Well, it was his father. When he died, Rupert took the old house over, but it was very reluctantly."

"Really? I thought he left the army to do it."

"No," said Joan, shaking her head firmly. "He left the army and he took over the house but there was no connection. Rupert would probably have preferred a desk job with his regiment, or something at the Imperial War Museum. But he felt he had no choice. He was the best of a bad bunch by far."

"What was wrong with the rest of the family?"

"Skinflints. Money-grubbers."

"Didn't save them enough to save the house."

"Incompetent money-grubbers, then."

"Which wing of the family?"

"Both. But the Fienneses were a bit less blatant and a bit less incompetent than the Quarleses."

"I see. Sir Stafford is one of that bunch. He's the chairman of the Trust."

"And doesn't everybody know it! He's a very junior sprig, and so far as is known, he's fairly straight, fairly knowledgeable too. Still, I wouldn't trust him as far as I could throw him."

"How did the transfer of the house from one branch to the other come about?"

"Ha! Everybody in the village wishes they knew. It's something the Fienneses didn't want to talk about, and the Quarleses were no longer around to talk."

"I've never heard anything about the personalities involved. It was just before war broke out, wasn't it?"

"Just after, I think. Anyway 1939. The Quarleses had been heads of the family for centuries. The elder son of the house was killed in the trenches in the First World War, and Timothy, the other son, was the survivor and he took over. He was mean he was incompetent."

"I see," said Felicity thoughtfully. "Of course a lot of

aristocratic and gentry families did give up the unequal struggle with the tax man about that time."

"Yes. But people say it would have been better if Timmy had done just that, rather than struggling and sinking deeper and deeper into the mire."

"Was he a wastrel—breaking the family mold?"

"Oh, no. He was typical. He had a variety of clever wheezes to make money, most of them dismal failures. The last one was started in the thirties, and it was a series of seminars, as they called them—making it sound very respectable and intellectually stimulating."

Felicity was for the first time puzzled. "What do you mean? English-literature seminars? A sort of adult-education thing?"

"No. Much more specialized than that. Today we'd call them peace studies. Lectures on the economic consequences of the peace treaty of Versailles, on the theory and practice of pacifism, and so on. I think the really important thing was the people they attracted. The seminars took place at least twice a year. They attracted names and money, and also creative people— poets, painters, musicians—so there was a highly presti- gious blend of intellectual brilliance and simple dosh. It worked, for once in Timmy's little life."

"But what's the connection—"

"Between that and the sale? Heaven only knows. Country manors and stately homes were going on the market all the time, so my mother says. It could just be a normal transaction: Timmy found that the peace sem- inars were not enough to keep his head above water, in spite of all the names and the moneybags, and he found that the junior branch, the Fienneses, were interested in buying. It may have been as simple as that."

"Simple is the best," said Felicity.

"Agreed," said Joan. "People in Walbrook, however, don't associate either the Fienneses or the Quarleses with simplicity. They are both looked at with—well, I think *suspicion* is the right word."

"Interesting." Felicity tried a long shot. "You say you still have good contacts at Walbrook?"

"Pretty good. Of course the generation that knew it in the thirties is dying out. But there are plenty of people who knew the situation at what we might call good secondhand. I mean the sort of people who heard a lot about the two branches of the family from their parents, friends, and so on."

"So you could give me a list of likely contacts I could talk to—starting with your mother, maybe?"

"I could make a list, but I'm not sure I'd start with my mother. Her memories are going—you know, I'm sure, that names and dates are among the first things to go, as often as not, and it's certainly so in my mother's case. She would be bewildered by a strange face, and that would drive more things out of her mind. I think it would be better if I tried to get memories out of her: she'll be less flummoxed. I could concentrate on the seminars and the transfer of power to the Fienneses, maybe."

"Brilliant. I'll be in your debt. I look forward to seeing the list of possible contacts too."

Felicity felt highly satisfied with her morning's work. That evening over dinner (rendered even later than usual by their daughter's demand to be taught how to do joined-up writing), Felicity and Charlie went over all she had learned that day about the peace seminars, the people at Walbrook, the transfer of the house, and so on. Charlie didn't let the conversation interfere with his healthy appetite, but he cataloged and arranged in his mind all the information Felicity gave him.

When he had finished eating, he sat looking at the tablecloth. "Those seminars."

"Yes?"

"I'm probably going off on a tangent. I remember reading, probably in the *Guardian,* or maybe *History Today*—"

"When do you see *History Today?*"

"DC Portland subscribes, and his desk is next to mine. I sometimes pinch it during lunch break. They had an article about a historian—a pretty well-known one, I think, maybe even a popularizer—who wrote a book about Hitler in the thirties, praising him to the skies. I think it was published sometime in 1934, and when war broke out, he went to some lengths to retrieve any copies that could be bought back and destroyed. He also used his influence to prevent newspapers and journals printing any reviews—favorable or unfavorable. He wanted to turn it into a nonbook, and he largely succeeded."

"You're beginning to ring a few bells."

"The book was never to be mentioned in interviews, which would be a natural thing to do: 'How did you come to be fooled by an obvious murderous lunatic'—so why the kid-glove treatment? What had he done to earn it?"

"Bryant," said Felicity. "Sir Arthur Bryant. That was his name. Interesting that. The why and the when need to be looked at. I have the impression he went on writing books with a true-blue Englishman slant for years—decades—after the war. Books with titles like *English Saga* and *Unfinished Victory*. But before that it was *The Man and the Hour*—and you can guess who 'the man' was."

"That's the historian I read about. Bryant. Not perhaps holier-than-thou but definitely more patriotic-than-thou. A very good vanishing trick with the book. It may be hardly anyone knew anything about it, except close friends." Charlie paused for a second helping of Irish stew. "And then there's Neville Chamberlain," he said at last.

"What's he got to do with it?"

"Went to negotiate with Hitler over his virtual annexation of a large part of Czechoslovakia. Flew to Munich in September 1938. Came back waving a bit of bog paper and pronouncing 'Peace in our time' with 'Guess who done it' as a silent addendum. Massive crowds in the Mall shouted their enthusiasm, and the king and queen took him out onto the Buckingham Palace balcony."

"Rather unwillingly on their part, I would guess," said Felicity.

"Yes, because war came within a year and he stayed on as prime minister, but his conduct of the war and of the civilian response was so feeble that people wondered which side he was on. Eventually one of his own MPs told him, 'In the name of God, go,' and that's what he did, conveniently dying soon after, so everyone could forget him and concentrate on Churchill."

"The moral of all this is?" asked Felicity.

"That what in 1937 or '38 was commendable, even patriotic, by 1939 or '40 seemed close to treason."

Felicity nodded gravely. "I get your point. And in 1939, around the time war broke out, the manor house of Walbrook changed hands."

"Staying within the family," said Charlie, nodding in his turn, "but going to a minor branchlet who had at that time enough money to buy it outright and later to expunge 'Hitler's pal' Timmy Quarles."

"What were they afraid of?" Felicity wondered.

"Or what was the man who bought it afraid of? In its way the disappearance of the seminars from popular—or even historians'—consciousness was as big an achievement as the vanishing trick the historian Bryant played with his book."

"It reminds me of Sir Anthony Eden," said Felicity. "After the Suez invasion he resigned as prime minister 'for medical reasons,' and also did a disappearing act, while Harold Macmillan became prime minister. He stayed on until he had his own medical reasons for going, then remained in the national consciousness as a sort of upper-crust music-hall act."

"The frustrating thing is that nothing seems to connect," said Charlie thoughtfully. "We have a plan to write a song cycle with an antiwar twist and several composers. Good publicity, good appeal to the sort of pacifist who calls on patriotic as well as conscientious motivations: the slaughter was terrible; would anyone really want to inflict that on our exhausted country for a second time twenty years later? And when the answer turned out to be yes, a swift about-turn had to be executed."

"Politicians are used to doing that. Probably that's why people are staying away from the polls at election time. You don't know what you're voting for."

"True. Now there's one thing worries me," said Charlie, sitting back in his chair, his meal finished.

"What's that?"

"You're on the way to getting a list of local people who might have information on the house and family, stretching back to the thirties. But you can't guarantee the truth of local gossip. Any policeman could tell you that much of it is rubbish—one person after another getting hold of the wrong end of the stick."

"I can't say I'm surprised. How, after all, would the locals *know*, if the family at the manor was congenitally secretive?"

"There you are—spot-on. That's why I'd be sad to see you concentrating too much on local yokels—to put it rudely."

"What's the alternative?"

"Well, you've got two possible alternative sources. You've got Sir Stafford, and you've got everyone's favorite grandee."

"Rupert Fiennes, do you mean? Yes, I'd like to talk the whole business over with him. He strikes me as basically reliable."

"Don't," said Charlie emphatically. "Don't go into this with preconceptions about people, particularly people

you hardly know. And remember that each of those two people has an accompanying figure. Sir Stafford has a wife, and Rupert has—what is she, a sort of cousin? Or a niece, or great-niece?"

"Don't know. Never met her."

"Lived with the Fienneses for years, so presumably she's one of them rather than one of the Quarleses. Presumably good relations between Rupert and Mary-Elizabeth—"

"Is that her name? How did you know?"

"I put my policeman's hat on. We've got a rookie constable at the Leeds HQ who was brought up in Walbrook. Anyway, let's get this straight: if you go into this on the assumption that Rupert is straight as a die and Stafford is a crook, you're asking for a fall. It's the amateur cop's first lesson. And similarly, don't get the idea that the jaundiced interpretation of the locals is bound to be more reliable than the family's own version of what happened. 'It ain't necessarily so.'"

"'The things that yo' li'ble to read in the Bible.' That's all very well, but we haven't actually *got* a Bible version of events yet."

"One piece of information, possibly true, possibly of interest: it's said around Walbrook—according to my infant PC—that Mary-Elizabeth Fiennes is going to join the board of the Walbrook Trust."

"Really? She and Rupert both. Is Sir Stafford agreeable?"

"Apparently. So that knocks on the head any idea that this is a last battle of the Fienneses and the Quarleses."

"Perhaps there never was a battle," said Felicity.

"You'll be able to judge when you go to your first board meeting. It could be a revelation."

"It could be. But I doubt the revelation will come from Sir Stafford."

Charlie sighed. "You haven't been listening to me, Fel."

Felicity remembered this the next day when she was pushing her son, Thomas, through the main street of Halifax and saw coming toward her Maya Tyndale similarly encumbered with little Theo. They stopped outside the Public Library and settled down for a natter.

"Ready for Saturday?" asked Maya.

"I suppose so," said Felicity. "I don't know what the meeting of a Trust should be like. I've read all the papers we've been sent, and there doesn't seem to be anything of any great importance."

"The oldest trick in the book. You then smuggle the vital thing you want to have decided your way into the committee's discussions under Any Other Business and say it's just come up and a decision needs to be taken at the meeting, and here is some more paperwork on it . . ."

"Yes, I know that kind of crookery from university meetings. Can't we demand that we be given the papers before lunch and read them over the break so we're alert to what he's doing?"

"You can try. I met Mary-Elizabeth Fiennes, and she said Stafford was hoping to get away before lunch. You knew Mary-Elizabeth was coming on the board, didn't you?"

"I did, on the grapevine. But I don't know *her*."

"She's okay, I think. Knows a lot about the family—*too* family-orientated on the whole, but at heart I think she's a fairly good egg."

"If matters before the board relate to the past—the family's past, the house's past—then someone with a lot of knowledge could be valuable. I don't get any sense of history from Rupert."

"Oh, no. I've always found that. No interest there at all. In fact I've seen the tape of an interview he gave on television—*Look North*—and when he talks about the house's history, the family's importance in the district, I could just hear Mary-Elizabeth's voice coming through over and over again. She'd been feeding him. They were her words."

"What did he say?"

"Oh, apart from the known facts of the family history, there wasn't much to the point. It came through that he was jolly keen to get rid of the estate."

"Didn't mention the seminars in the thirties?"

"No. I don't know much about them myself. He did mention that the house had strong connections over the years with the world of music, and as the new Trust had decided to have a small, unpretentious music festival there, the record of the earlier times, the seminars, would be invaluable."

"Really? I shouldn't have thought that things that happened seventy-odd years ago could be very relevant today. Most of the performers and composers would be long dead by now."

"I suppose so," said Maya, wrinkling her forehead. "Except the organizers would probably have gone for the younger people in the music world back in the thirties. Cheaper. They could be still around, or some of them."

"True. And it would be the younger people in the world of politics that they'd have wanted to attract to the seminars too. Ah, well—wait and see. Charlie says I'm too prone to take a side and assign all the virtues to my side and all the vices to the other."

"I suppose he's got all the virtues of a policeman."

"Oh, absolutely. When the good fairy came to his christening one of the gifts she gave him was that of being totally noncommittal. Invaluable for a policeman, infuriating for everyone else."

CHAPTER 6

Charitable Trust

✳

The January meeting of the Walbrook Trust Board took place as usual in the house's stable block. Attractive from the outside, it turned out to be of the utmost mediocrity inside: a table, chairs, a little kitchen extension—that was about it. A modest plaque said that the conversion of the building was made possible by a generous donation from Barland Woolf Biscuits Ltd. On the table by the door to the kitchenette were tea- and coffeepots, cups and saucers, and a large plate of biscuits, no doubt a generous donation from Barland Woolf Ltd.

Felicity was beginning to get to know the existing members of the Trust Board. She was ready-armed when Janet Porritt steamed up, her face showing a mask of false friendship identical to that she had worn at the reception weeks earlier. She was one of a body of people Felicity had long ago identified: those who believed Anglo-Saxons should only marry Anglo-Saxons. The more boring the world could be, the better they liked it. Smile, damn you, she said to herself.

"Oh, Mrs. Peace. Good to see you again, and among us too—one of us! I hope your husband has forgiven me for wondering why he was at our little concert."

"Of course he has. He gets such questions all the time."

"I suppose all policemen do."

"Yes, they do. It can be useful if people come to him with things that are relevant to his job. But he *was* off duty that night, and nobody came to him with anything."

"No, I'm sure they didn't. We are utterly open in everything we do . . . So young to be an inspector. He must be very talented. He's not from Yorkshire of course?"

"No, London—he's really a Cockney, but there's not much left of it in his accent or language. That's because he lives with me, I suppose. I'm mostly West Country, and only the people he works with are for the most part Yorkshire men and women."

"Well, maybe you could both learn a bit of the brogue, and you'll soon be accepted and naturalized. Please do remember me to him!"

She steamed off, obviously satisfied that she had double-stamped the Peaces as foreigners, and not likely to become honorary Yorkshiremen unless considerable changes were made.

"Silly old cow!" said a voice to Felicity's left.

She turned around. "Oh—we met at the concert, didn't we?" she said, smiling at someone she thought of as a kindred soul. "Teacher—am I right? And an Irish name—Hooley, wasn't it? And Ben? Irish, but not particularly Irish. Long residence here? Or maybe a feeling it's best not to flaunt it?"

"Don't let Poisonous Porritt influence you too much. All sorts get on pretty well together here. I'm Ben because my parents liked the name. And because I was the youngest in the family—a late mistake."

"Ah. I'm not too good on the Bible."

"The Irish are. Not that they take much notice of it."

"My father's only religion was the worship of himself. I had my work cut out resisting that without troubling myself with the Bible."

"Yorkshire not so long ago was a county of the Bible-thumper, but my parents were at the end of that movement, and by the time they died they couldn't be dragged to church, except in a coffin."

"So what sort of trick is our revered chairman going to pull today? I've been warned about matters that he introduces at the last moment."

"Oh, that's a trick that every chairman keeps up his sleeve. Some of the craftier kind have follow-ups to the last-minute ploy. Oh, there are all sorts of games you can play when it's you is running the meeting."

"You don't have respect for your great leader?"

"On the contrary, I have a great respect for him. He's 'passing honest' by the standards of his kind. If you stop him in his tracks, he accepts he's been checkmated and he goes away and thinks up something else. Most of his tricks are either well-known or easily perceived with the naked eye."

"The thing I ask myself," said Felicity, "is 'What is the motivation?' People tell me what he has done, but they never tell me why he has done it."

"Remember," said Ben Hooley, becoming serious,

"he isn't just a distinguished outsider—a distinguished museum person, though he is that—called in to midwife a new Trust through its infancy. He's a member of the family—maybe that should be plural, families—who owned the house. Perhaps he sees this as a kind of Restoration: King Charles the Second returning to his own country to take up the reins of power again. At any rate if the idea gets around that he is the head of the family, that he is the resident of Walbrook Manor, that the board is primarily a rubber stamp for his decisions—"

"He won't go round denying it."

"Exactly. Whoops! Here we go."

Sir Stafford had been knocking rather feebly on the table in front of him. He somehow didn't look like a conspirator. Little knots of board members began drifting to their places where their piles of papers had been set out. Sir Stafford began to speak—his voice more powerful than his knocking.

"We must get on. . . . There's plenty to do, but first of all, let me welcome two new members. Felicity Peace is a published novelist and a literary scholar with several learned papers to her name, on Christopher Isherwood and Elizabeth Taylor—I presume that is *not* the well-known one but the much-praised novelist who is no longer with us. Let me also welcome Mary-Elizabeth Fiennes, Rupert's . . . er, cousin, and someone you all know because she is absolutely *the* expert on the house which is at the heart of the Trust, and the family, which is hardly less important."

Felicity looked at Mary-Elizabeth. She saw a smallish woman, probably into her seventies, taking off her rimless spectacles and looking around the room with a nervous smile on her face. Two or three decades ago a man might have said "typical brown owl," but Felicity disliked generalizations designed to malign by ridicule. She quite liked what she saw.

"Thank you very much," Mary-Elizabeth said. "I don't know how I am to live up to that. But I do admit to being fascinated by the house, and also the family. But we are all interested in our families, aren't we?"

I'm not, thought Felicity. But I suppose everyone would be shocked if I said it out loud.

"I just know that when I have a problem," said Sir Stafford, "Mary-Elizabeth is the person I go to. Now, we have a crowded morning of discussion, and I have another matter, newly come up, to add to the Any Other Business agenda, so if we can make a start . . ."

"Mr. Chairman," said Felicity, "if this new matter is coming up towards the end of the meeting, could we know what it is now, and have any papers associated with it, so that we can read them in the coffee break?"

Sir Stafford looked surprised and perhaps a little obstinate. "Oh, I don't think that's necessary. The item is not of major importance. Now, first item, minutes of the last meeting—"

"Mr. Chairman," said Ben Hooley, waving a fist, "I'd like to associate myself with Mrs. Peace's suggestion. If we can't have what little advance notice there can be now, I'd like my objection to be recorded in the minutes."

"Mine too," said Felicity.

"Mr. Gannett is taking the minutes. He will no doubt

notice your objection and suggestion, and my reply. That's the way we do things here. Now, in the minutes of the last meeting, that of November twelfth of last year . . ."

Felicity sat biting her lip, resenting the way he had treated her—as if she were a clueless schoolgirl who had no idea how meetings should be conducted. They trudged through the minutes pointing out every misplaced inverted comma, every obvious typo, struggling manfully and womanfully over the smallest inconsistency. They went on to report progress on all matters that would mark the first proper opening of the house as a museum and exhibition gallery. Bookings for the education program were most encouraging, all the exhibits and photographs for the First World War exhibition now called *Life in the Trenches* had arrived, and Wes Gannett reported on his efforts to install them in time for the opening, and on the recruitment of the volunteer staff to ensure the safety both of the items on loan to the exhibition and the pictures and furniture that belonged to the house. The information purveyed to the board got more and more trivial, and the likelihood of the meeting being short enough to end before lunch became more and more unlikely. Finally they got to Any Other Business.

"Ah, yes, this is that little matter I mentioned," said Sir Stafford, riffling idly through some sheets of paper he had retrieved from his files. "It is the matter of Dr. Turnbull, who was voted onto the board several months ago—I think in July of last year. Most of you will have been here then . . ."

He looked around the little group, and some nodded like glove puppets.

"She's not here today," Ben Hooley pointed out.

"No—and that is rather the point. This is the third meeting in a row Dr. Turnbull has missed. She has sent the usual forms of excuse, but the truth is she has missed every chance to take up her seat with us and to become *au fait* with what we are doing. The latest letter pleads silver-wedding celebrations involving a cousin and his wife and is one of Dr. Turnbull's 'long-standing commitments.' I should have thought we were qualified for her attention under the same heading. I have tried to set up a meeting with her, but to no avail. The fact is we have put on the board someone whom nobody knows—is that right?" Sir Stafford looked around the table.

"I think I've met her," said Ben Hooley. "Passing handshake is all."

"She is one of my patients," said a fresh-faced man whom Felicity had identified as Dr. Cullingworth. "She's never ill. Best kind of patient: just a number with nothing wrong with her. A statistic only."

"This all does underline what I've said," said Sir Stafford. "We have put on the board someone whom nobody knows, and who knows none of us. I fear the fault is primarily mine, and I do, naturally, apologize for recommending the lady. I suggest we remove her quietly and write suggesting that we need active members of the board, and we recommend that she postpone joining up until her work and private life allow her time to take a full part in our decision-making processes."

"But what if she doesn't accept your suggestion and decides to remain a member?" demanded Janet Porritt. "As far as I can see, that is *her* decision, not ours. We must be more careful in the future."

"In the Charity Commission's booklet there are situations gone into that might be used if it was thought—" began Maya Tyndale. But she had awoken dim memories in Sir Stafford, who now began rummaging in his papers and finally came up with a green booklet, which he waved, crowing.

"Here it is. 'If he or she is absent for all meetings held over a period of six months, his or her membership can be declared invalid—' Got her! . . . Sorry, that was unsympathetic. But we can activate this provision and get ourselves a more useful member."

"Hmmm," said Ben Hooley. "Shouldn't be difficult. Her expertise is history with particular emphasis on the twentieth century, as I vaguely recall. No, shouldn't be a problem there."

"I don't think that we should lay emphasis on the twentieth century," said Sir Stafford in his most querulous tones. "That only applied to this year, with the *Life in the Trenches* exhibition going on. Say next year or the year afterward our exhibition is on eighteenth-century portraiture—if our reputation is good enough by then to get people to lend us their pictures—then we'd need some other sort of expertise. We want someone broad-ranging, or with the contacts and expertise to allow him, or her, naturally, to recommend someone we could use on an ad hoc basis."

"We'll give you discretion," said Janet Porritt in her

most fawning tones, "on how to approach Dr. Turnbull. You have so much experience in tricky situations. It's invaluable."

And on that cozy note of anal-licking the meeting broke up, with Felicity and other sympathetic members feeling they had been led into colluding in something dubiously legal and faintly discreditable. But why Sir Stafford should want what they had just decided stumped them. Over coffee in the manor's cafeteria, Felicity, Ben Hooley, and Wes Gannett churned over the decision.

"I don't get it," Felicity said. "Presumably Sir Stafford was in on the decision to ask this Dr. Turnbull to stand. Now he's changed his mind and wants the appointment taken away from her, without giving her a chance to respond. He has had virtually no contact with her, nor she with any of us. Maybe her reasons for missing the meetings have been stronger than they appear. What has changed Sir Stafford's view of the job, the person, the current situation?"

"Ah," said Gannett. "I think I could make a guess at that."

"Go on," said Hooley.

"When you set up a trust, you aim to get balance. You want a selection of the people who might have expertise that will make them of use: in this case architectural and artistic knowledge presumably with a good academic title behind it. Then maybe a historian, as now, an actual builder, one specializing in historic buildings, someone with museum experience, and so on. So that's what Sir Stafford went for in the beginning—had to go for, rather than just appointing a number of cronies he'd gained in the course of a long life spent in museums."

"I see that," said Felicity. *"And?"*

"And once the trust is set up, all the preliminary work is done and so forth, a few significant changes can be made, and the board can be turned into what it should not be—a coven of cronies."

"Unquestionably approving whatever Sir Stafford chooses to do?" suggested Ben Hooley.

"Exactly."

"And what does Sir Stafford want his poodles *for?*" asked Felicity.

Wes Gannett shrugged. "I've no idea, or nothing concrete. The old boy would keep whatever it may be well away from me. It could be something quite ordinary and simple, with no sinister overtones. It could be just pocket money from something or other—say the song cycle we heard at the concert. Remember, Sir Stafford is not paid to be the chairman of the board. He's got the flat for a rent that is hardly more than peanuts, but that is presumably only until the museum is firmly established—say another year or so."

"But the song cycle would be 'forever'—or at least well beyond Sir Stafford's death," said Ben Hooley.

"Yes. But remember that officially it belongs to the Trust. And remember that songs and song cycles are not the most marketable things in the world—unlike symphonies, concertos, if they are by 'names.' Play a song cycle a couple of times on Radio Three, program it for a Prom concert, interest one or two of the regional orchestras in it—and that's about it, unless it's a masterpiece with a life stretching out to infinity. I'm no expert, but it didn't sound to me as if that was the case."

They looked at each other, still unsure whether they were onto something. Then they downed their coffees and left the little cafeteria, wondering if Sir Stafford regarded them too as "poodles."

When she had said good-bye to Wes and Ben, Felicity took herself for a walk around the grounds of Walbrook. A healthy sprinkling of families were visiting the manor, and several solemn single visitors, looking as if they were casing the joint to see if it was worth a visit next time Auntie Mary came to stay. It was a quarter to two. The manor and grounds would surely lose some of their visitors when the lunch hour was over. Slowly, and still mulling over the possibilities for fraud presented by the house and its contents, many of which, she suspected, had as yet not been assessed or cataloged, Felicity pointed her steps in the direction of the house. At the top of the incline she could see families walking away or getting into their cars, some of the solitary ones going back to work, others, she guessed, aiming for a pub lunch. She turned, satisfied, and went into the house.

Inside what was now called somewhat overstatedly the Great Hall was a small shop, where people were buying postcards and picture books, fridge magnets and pictorial mugs. When they had been relieved of their money, they drifted through the main door and down

to the car park by the stables. The house was empty-
ing nicely. Felicity paid her entrance fee, smiled at the
attendant's comment that she had every right to go
in free, then walked briskly through the ground-floor
rooms. She made note of any small changes since she'd
last seen them, mostly new placement of pictures and
adjustments to the accompanying labels. Then she went
back to the Hall and mounted the stairs.

The first sight that met her eyes was a giant picture
on the landing wall of ten or twelve soldiers under
bombardment in a trench. She immediately wanted to
turn away: the men's eyes had a look of sheer mental
shutdown, of being no longer in the world. Peering into
one or two rooms, she saw photographs from the Allied
front where she glimpsed men with the same terrible
symptoms of war-sickness. She glanced quickly into all
the rooms, then went back to the top of the stairs: the
first floor was devoid of visitors.

There was no point in delaying a decision: she had
come up the stairs hoping to find this floor empty,
which would enable her to slip up to the attic. At the
end of one of the corridors, a poky staircase had a rope
stretched across its lower steps with a sign saying NO
ADMITTANCE. She marched quickly toward it, put the
rope aside and then back across the entrance when she
was on the lower steps. Carefully she made her way up
the stairs, then through the door at the top. She felt
for a light switch and found one: the musty attic was at
once illuminated by a dim light. . . . Gradually the power
increased: the attic was lit by new age bulbs.

To her right there was open space: a near-empty

floor area with only two small trunks, odd pages of printed paper (wrapping perhaps from a printer or a publisher), and opened envelopes and balls of paper. On the other side of the entrance door the sloping roof had been enclosed with a moderately secure-looking wooden wall—three storage rooms, thought Felicity, each with a door. Quietly she trod along the dusty corridor and tried each of the doors: no luck, except that by the doorknob of each of the locked rooms and cupboards was a square of paper, each with a letter on it. First *W*, second *Q*, third *F*. Felicity didn't waste much time on them: the *W* and the *Q* told her that this must be for Walbrook itself and the two families who had ruled from here over the local tenantry and farmers for several hundred years.

She thought suddenly that she had seen enough, had risked her place on the board sufficiently, and it was time to go. She switched off the light and crept down the stairway. From the lower steps she saw a couple disappearing into one of the rooms in the *Life in the Trenches* exhibition. She watched them go in, then let herself back into the public part of the house. Looking up the central corridor she saw the door to the Quarleses' grace-and-favor flat. So near and yet so far!

She slipped down the Grand Staircase and out into the fresh air. A few yards away from her, on the path leading to the car park, was Mary-Elizabeth Fiennes. She was walking in a discontented, almost resentful posture, and when Felicity caught up with her, she thought she saw tears on her face.

"Hello," she said, feeling she should be a little bit formal. "I'm Felicity Peace. We didn't really get a chance to get acquainted this morning."

Mary-Elizabeth brushed her cheeks. "Oh . . . Hello. Stafford isn't very good at making sure that we know each other, is he? I used to live here, you know."

"And have found it rather a strain coming back, I should think."

Mary-Elizabeth's head was nodding vigorously. "Yes! Isn't it silly to be surprised? That was bound to be how I felt. I'd been living in the house since I was a child. I suppose it's natural that I feel a terrible wrench. I loved the house, and the fact that it was owned by my cousin's father and then by my cousin was part of its attraction. I was always reminding Rupert that he was lord of the manor and getting him up to scratch, urging him to do the decent thing. Sometimes I was successful, sometimes not."

"He didn't have the same family feeling, then?"

"No, he didn't. I don't know why not. Whenever I pulled out the lord-of-the-manor card, he said that as far as he knew, there was no such title, he had taken the manor over from his father with the utmost reluctance, and he would be much happier if the house was open to the public and he could move out to a comfortable flat with all mod cons. He and I, I should say. He always said that one way or other I would have a home for life, and he'd make it clear in his will that that was always to be the case."

"That was very generous, and very considerate too. Shows he does have some family feeling, doesn't it?"

"Yes. But for the people, not for the house."

"Yes, I suppose so," said Felicity, thinking that Rupert had got things the right way round.

Mary-Elizabeth had said it in a way that suggested she was nourishing her discontent. They had reached the car park and Felicity tried to detain the rather elfin elderly lady.

"Well, we'll be seeing quite a lot of each other, won't we? I wondered if I could do a bit of research on the family and the house."

"Oh, you'd have to square that with Stafford, not me."

"I suppose so. I don't know any reason why he should object."

"I often don't see any reason behind what Stafford does," said Mary-Elizabeth, her voice a genteel dagger.

"I just want to see the documents of the house—what work was done when and by whom, relations with tenant farmers—that kind of thing."

"I used to be the unofficial and inefficient secretary to the place, and I filed all documents like that in my own ineffable system."

"Where were they kept?"

"Periodically I'd have a great big clear-out of the study and take piles of documents and less official papers to file away."

"Nothing scandalous in them? Things Sir Stafford might not want me to see?"

"Nothing scandalous for the last I-don't-know-how-long. As a family we just didn't go in for scandalous doings. You'll be hard put to it to find anything at all, apart from Sir Richard and his Arabella in the 1760-somethings."

"So you think Sir Stafford will let me see the files?"

"No idea. If he doesn't, I can tell you how to get a look at the documents about the house."

"Really?"

"If they're still where I left them, I can."

"In the attic."

"Exactly."

"But the doors will be locked, surely?"

"They will, almost certainly. They were when I left the house. Stafford asked about the keys and I gave him the duplicate set."

"And the other set?"

"Just ask and I'll tell you. I may even come with you for a look around the old place. Cheery pip!"

And she raised her hand and marched off to the small Honda car that had nothing to distinguish it from the other cars in the car park except that it was much more dirty. Felicity got into her car with nagging feelings of dissatisfaction. Why had Mary-Elizabeth seemed so eager to get away? She had taken flight—had she also taken fright? Why? What was there in the—

Then Felicity remembered. She had started to talk about keys to the offices in the attic when she should not have shown any sign of knowing about the unusual setup there in the top of the house. Yet Mary-Elizabeth had seemed so willing to lead her to the main set of keys, even if Sir Stafford objected. Felicity shook her head and started the car: she was not in a position to understand the strange proclivities of the landed gentry of Yorkshire. And in the normal course of events she would not have felt any need to make herself *au fait* with them. Now, however, she felt a certain shiver of excitement at the prospect of discovering family secrets.

As she drove out into the open road, she heard music and thought it came from a nearby cottage. She reminded herself that there were members of the Fiennes family whom she had yet to meet.

CHAPTER 7

Gossip

✳

A few weeks after the board meeting Felicity made her next real advance. She had driven to Walbrook with some paperwork needed to make her appointment to the board official—having decided that delivering it at HQ in person had the advantage that it would also provide opportunities to sticky beak on what was going on, only a week or so ahead of the longer opening hours of the manor. She left the car in the stables' car park and began a leisurely walk up to the old house, which looked wonderful in the watery sun.

The lawns also looked wonderful—stretching from house to road and to the stables and the Dower House below. They were dotted with visitors, but also by a little group of men not far from Felicity's path, each one presumably master of a dog—because there were six dogs to the six men. Felicity recognized a rottweiler, a Weimaraner, a border terrier, and assorted mongrels who made no apology for their lack of a family tree. The dogs were making a great concerted rush every time a ball was thrown from an owner's experienced arm, traveling farther than she would have guessed possible. The dogs' only respite from this joyful race was when they went off to do a squat followed by their rightful owner, with a little black bag. Felicity decided that if she stayed long enough, she would be able to pair each dog and each owner.

The owners were mostly pensioners, many with the swaying paunch of the insufficiently occupied. The youngest, in his fifties or sixties most probably, was as wide as he was short, as a result of taking steroids in his teens. He looked as if he would thoroughly enjoy anyone's daring to kick sand in his face. Another was trying to stir into action his chocolate-colored Labrador, who refused to join in the game and would only sit on the luxuriant grass, paws out front and head on paws, seeming to be shaking his head at the spectacle of dogs making gigantic fools of themselves. The beautifully groomed Weimaraner with a pink collar was being encouraged to run faster by its owner—tattooed arms and head, pink trousers, and a general air of wanting to be acknowledged as the natural heir to the character created by Kenneth Williams.

"Lovely day," shouted Felicity.

"All the better for seeing you, my love," said Pink Trousers. Felicity laughed and started over toward them.

"It's nice to see that you can use the grounds," she said. To her surprise there was a general burst of laughter. "What's funny about that?"

"It's no thanks to them that run this place," said the bodybuilder, whom Felicity christened in her mind

Cockles. "Old Stafford wanted the grounds restricted to people who'd paid the entrance fee to the house."

"You'd pay a fortune to police a regulation like that," said Felicity.

"Ah! A girl with brains. Course you would. It's just not worth trying, and as we mobilized the village against it, he didn't stand a chance. Typical rich man, all that fuss was, always looking for new ways to fleece the poor they are, and Old Stafford's no different."

"I thought Sir Stafford's branch of the family were pretty poor," Felicity said. "That's why they had to sell the house."

"Sell the house, my arse," said an elderly owner of a Doberman/rottweiler cross who, sleek, groomed, authoritarian, was competing to be the Warren Beatty of the dog world. "They sold it all right, but not because they were hard up."

"Why then?"

The question embarrassed the man. "Ah. The village never quite found out the details. Will here's dad was one of the lawnsmen back then, later head gardener, so what he learned he got from visitors who were willing to stroll in the grounds and gardens and spill the beans on what they'd heard in the house. That was pretty sensational, but not things you could pin down. Lots of people told him that the Quarleses were being blackmailed."

"By whom? About what?"

"By the Fienneses. Who else? They bought the house for a pittance and set themselves up here as soon as the war was over. What it was all about Will's dad never found out. All these old families have their guilty secrets, don't they? And not just one. It must have been something the Quarleses didn't want revealed and the Fiennes didn't care a damn about."

"Don't quote me on this," said an elderly man with a mongrel biting his shoelaces, and a red face that suggested that the pub tradition in Britain was not entirely dead, "but my grandmother was a housemaid at the manor, and the indoor servants all believed that there was something queer about these schools, or seminars, or whatever they were called. Something not quite right. You know about the seminars, before the war, young lady?"

"I've heard of them," said Felicity.

"What exactly do you mean by *queer*?" asked the owner of the pink-collared dog.

"Oh, nothing you could lose your cool over," said the elderly man, "though there was a contingent of your sort at most of the weekends. No, it was how the seminars were presented and the contrast with what they were actually intended to do."

"I don't get your drift."

"They were advertised as sessions for concerned people devoted to preventing what had happened twenty years before—the mass slaughter of the Great War."

"And what were they really?"

"A fifth column of Nazi sympathizers."

Felicity blinked. "But were there all that many of them?"

"Enough. Terrible things were heard by us villagers— welcomes for people who wouldn't stand any nonsense from 'those confounded Jews' and so on. A lot of the speakers at the seminars were literary people, artists too and musicians. They knew how to put across these people's aims, giving them a favorable and attractive coating, if you get my meaning. So it looked like a desperate plea—'Don't let's go back to that terrible time'—when in fact the seminar would be softening the attendees to go along with Hitler, give him all he demanded, including the mass murder of the Jews. Genocide wasn't yet the policy of Germany, but apparently it was in the air, and it came along pretty soon. And the fact that the First World War was a terrible waste of human life led people to listen."

"Sir Stafford was around all this time,' said Cockles, the square man with the muscles and tattoos. "He was here with his family all the time, in the lead-up to war."

"I know," said Felicity. "But he was about three years old when the war broke out. I don't think he can have been crucial in weakening Britain's resolve."

"His mother must have led to half the desertions from the British army," said Cockles. "She'd weaken any man's resolve, or so they said. A real Mata Hari, the oldies round here always maintained."

"I seem to have got the wrong end of the stick," said Felicity. "I was told she was an invalid, and she was here so she could go for treatment at Leeds General Infirmary. I think someone told me she died soon after the family went back to wherever was home for them."

"Maybe, maybe," said the man with the biggest paunch. "She may have been desperate to have a good time while she had the strength to enjoy it. There were rumors she was a patient of Dr. Owen Winstanley.

Name doesn't mean much nowadays, but at the time he was notorious."

"Oh, aye, he were," said the elderly man. "I remember after the war he was giving the National Health Service a bad name. They retired him quietly, so that he did his philandering as a private citizen."

"I heard she went to him once or twice a week while they were here," said Pink Trousers. "Apart from that, her time was her own. She used it well."

"Goodness!" said Felicity. "I have been learning things. I hope it's all a hundred percent reliable."

"Oh it is," said Paunch. "Walbrook village gossip is as near to cast-iron proof as you can get. The pope doesn't come near it for infallibility. And the 1930s was a first-rate vintage. You could take your oath on it."

"You're having me on," said Felicity, smiling. "I'll label it all in my mind as needing confirmation."

"As you please, lady," said Cockles, smiling back at her with—what was it? Felicity wasn't quite sure, but as she saw them all looking back at her and smiling, she thought it meant that they'd held back on one or two really appetizing morsels.

Up at the house the usual trickle of visitors was going from room to room, mostly in silence, but now and then breaking into cries of "Oh, look, Bill: it's a crystal set complete with earphones" or "My mother used to bake her scones in one of these." A museum such as Walbrook was a great feeder of nostalgia. She walked with a thoroughly proprietorial step up the stairs to the first floor. Nobody around. Too early in the morning for them to have exhausted the ground floor. Though the number of visitors was not so far impressive, their interest and absorption in the exhibits was cheering: she could see the audience appeal of Walbrook being deep and lasting.

She went along to the poky staircase and tiptoed up to the attic. The same dim light was on, and in it she saw Mary-Elizabeth waiting patiently, as she had promised to do on the phone. Her posture was friendly, as if she was pleased to be part of the action—whatever the action might be. She was part of the continuing story of the house, and a sort of historical guide.

"I didn't open up the doors," she said, "so you can see how to do it."

"I'm very grateful. You don't object if I come up here on my own if the opportunity presents itself?"

"Not at all. After all, we won."

Felicity blinked. "Sorry—who's 'we'?'

"The Fienneses, of course. I'm one of them by adoption. We were the goodies, there's no question of that. The Quarleses were up to all sorts of chicanery, but we were Persil white all along."

Felicity noted her dated partisanship and her equally dated vocabulary. She watched as Mary-Elizabeth unrolled a page of a glossy magazine. nicely stiff, and pushed it under the door marked W.

"I thought we'd want to start with the house," said Mary-Elizabeth. "I hope you agree?"

"Oh, yes, absolutely," said Felicity, noting Mary-Elizabeth's assumption that Felicity had already been up to the attic and guessed the significance of the initials on the doors. She watched as a small key emerged on the glossy pages of fashions and nightlife.

"Eureka!" said Mary-Elizabeth. "Who would have guessed?"

"Why did you need to do this? You said you have a key yourself."

"I thought we should change the system" was the reply, in a rather lady-of-the-manor voice. "I had the impression that Sir Stafford hadn't got a hope of investigating the archives yet awhile, and that we should have equal easy access. Just so that you, if you find you have one or two hours with nothing to fill them, can drop by and do a bit of snooping, without having to get a key from me and ask permission or anything."

"That sounds ideal," said Felicity, who was wondering if the mother of a ten-month-old ever had unexpectedly free time. "I appreciate it."

Mary-Elizabeth switched on the light in the tiny room. "Eureka! Or should that be abracadabra? More English." She giggled, like a schoolgirl.

Two small tables and chairs had been put against the sloping far wall, the inside of the roofing. At a gesture from Mary-Elizabeth, Felicity sat down and found herself sitting cheek by jowl with the representative of the Fiennes dynasty. They could look over each other's documents and their handling of them. She was not, Felicity thought, going to get much privacy today. Perhaps neither of them needed it. Perhaps they could work together.

"Now then: heigh-ho, heigh-ho, and all that," said the older woman. "I'm going to start with the financial situ-

ation of the Quarleses in the thirties. I've been wrestling
with it for Rupert for the last few years, and I'd like to go
deeper into how they got into their fix and how they got
out of it. What will you take?"

"I'd like to see how the peace seminars came into
being, and how they started being a moneymaking concern for the family of country-gentry folk who were
almost on the rocks."

"Good-oh. We're on related topics so we can chuck
over papers that relate also to the other's subject. Let
me see . . ."

Mary-Elizabeth got up, nearly bumping her head, and
peered along the rough shelves where a series of bulging
files were stored, each one labeled with an ill-written
description of its contents: her filing system was as dis-
organized as she had said. She took out two files from
the motley collection and banged down one on Felicity's
table and a second one on her own. Then with a grunt
she started reading from her own a series of bank state-
ments detailing the amounts of ready cash the family
had to play with in the thirties—not very much, so far as
Felicity could gather. She turned back to her own file,
which rejoiced in the label THE ROAD TO PEACE.

From the file's beginning, she knew she was not getting the facts behind the early years of the seminars. No
doubt that at some time Mary-Elizabeth had decided the
seminars deserved a file to themselves, but had not got
down to transferring the early filed documents.

"This file starts some way in," Felicity murmured to
her fellow worker. "After the first seminar."

"I thought it might, though I wasn't sure. For a while I

109

thought the whole thing was bogus and nonsensical, but I was quite pleased to have a subsection where I could file some things."

"Well, bung anything you get to me and I'll start afresh," said Felicity. Mary-Elizabeth grunted.

The first item in the file was a letter, one of four, which thanked Timothy Quarles for the "tremendous success" of the first seminar: "Bang-on as far as content was concerned, masses of things to make us think afresh, and plenty of like-minded people. I feel I've been talking nonstop for five days, and could start another seminar tomorrow with plenty left to say. Thanks again!"

The other letters were on similar lines, but one sentence caught Felicity's eye in the last letter she read: "Most important of all you had a sensible discussion of the new government in Germany and the importance of not making harsh judgments of Hitler and his cabinet before they have revealed their real (and possibly justified) aspirations for their country."

The letter was dated April 23, 1933.

Next was a jumble of bills, including meals served, domestic service rewarded, jobs for six or seven local women, then some records of payment sent to national and local newspapers for publicity. A memorandum noted that a request from a teachers' union that it be included in the house's mailing list had been rejected, on the ground that it involved the seminars' organizers becoming too close to one of the national political parties. The people putting together the seminars wrote a circular explaining why this policy was in place: it put them in a position not attached to any party but *above* them. They argued persuasively until you looked closely at some of the lecture titles and some of the topics covered in discussion. The jumble of paper then shifted to autumn 1933 and the explanation of the organization's aims: they projected three seminars, in spring, summer "during the school holidays," and autumn. Some names even eighty years later rang bells, and the organization was getting its feet under the table at Walbrook. The motive force was, insofar as it was spelled out, Timothy Quarles, and he had recruited a large pool of antiwar activists—most of these participated in the aims of the seminars and lectures, but one or two of them raised eyebrows even among the organizers: Oswald Mosley, leader of the British fascists was one such, and against his name were the words "No, or not yet." The financial basis of the seminars was illuminated by a draft letter to political speakers. Expenses would be paid, and of course meals and bed on the day of the talk. If the speaker wished to stay for the whole four-day conference (Friday to Monday) each extra meal was 17/6, the bedroom and bed was £2.10 a night, and it was hoped that all speakers would feel able to donate a little more of their time so as to participate in the delegates' chat after sessions, which was often the most stimulating part of the event.

"Here," said Mary-Elizabeth, slapping down a bundle of paper. "This is all I've got so far, probably all there is. It starts in 1929 with the germ of an idea and goes on to 1932. Then it was beginning to be seen as a political statement. That is, 'No war,' and you can see how it would have had an appeal after the slaughter of the Great War, can't you?"

"Yes," said Felicity, and she flicked through the papers. "I can see the appeal to intellectuals and artistic people. Lots of names who rang bells then, including some that still ring bells today. Siegfried Sassoon, Ralph Vaughan Williams, Robert Graves, William Walton, Edmund Blunden, and so on. No guarantee that all, or any, of these people came to Walbrook. Ivor Gurney is mentioned here, but he was in an asylum by then. Looking at the lists you've got a pretty good selection of the political, the *bien-pensant,* and the artistic. You've got to admit that Timmy Quarles did a pretty good job."

"I can't see how he solved his financial problems through raking in the fairly small sums mentioned here," said Mary-Elizabeth, dismissive as usual of the Quarles branch of the family.

"No," said Felicity. But she skipped through the remaining mountain of material in the peace-seminar file. "It was still going great guns in 1938 and '9. You'd think it was a lot of hard work for very little return—very little good, solid financial return, I mean. Unless—"

She regretted the word as soon as it was out of her mouth. She remembered Charlie's strictures about amateur investigators who acted on the assumption that one lot of people were the good guys leaving the other lot of people as the bad guys. Really she knew very little about Rupert Fiennes's cousin. But she needn't have worried. Mary-Elizabeth had made a minor discovery.

"Well, I didn't know that Timmy Quarles had an illegitimate daughter."

This seemed to give her more pleasure than any suggestion from Felicity was likely to do. She threw Felicity an ambiguous smile, but was soon submerged once again in her papers, and Felicity decided to ignore the intriguing statement and let her mind go back to the possibility she had been toying with. Unless, she had come close to saying, the seminars were being subsidized by a fairly hefty rake-in from some foreign power.

Felicity had been working for two hours and was thinking it was time to pack up and go home. As she reached to close her exercise book, a name that had already been mentioned jumped out from the collection of letters she had been working on.

"Oh, I say . . . Good heavens, it's the song cycle again. The one we heard before Christmas in the concert here."

"I've never been quite sure what a song cycle is," said Mary-Elizabeth.

"It's a series of songs that are connected in some way; usually they either have a story or they illustrate some theme. Like the one here was on the subject of wars, and the poems were mostly by First World War poets."

Mary-Elizabeth pouted. "I've no time for music. I think I've got a defective ear for it."

"This is interesting though," insisted Felicity. "It's a carbon copy—do you remember them?"

"Just about. More trouble than they were worth."

"Anyway the letter's to a man called Maurice Matlock, and it hails the fact that the cycle is nearly in its final form, says it could be enormously influential, says how good it will be to have a contribution from 'the late Ivor Gurney,' and asks if it would be possible to give a premiere—or at least a preview so to speak—of the cycle at the October seminar. 'I know Peter Pears is interested in singing one of the parts, though Ben has not come up with a contribution as yet.' Then the letter is signed 'Timothy Quarles.'"

Mary-Elizabeth gave an uninterested nod and was turning back to her accounts and receipts when the pair of them heard a creak. They looked at each other, Felicity frowning. Faint footsteps continued to the top of the stairs, then were heard, louder, on the attic floor. Slowly the handle of the door turned, then the door began slowly to open.

It was Lady Quarles.

"Oh, dear, I'm so sorry, Mary-Elizabeth. I had no idea you were up here. And, er, Felicity."

"Just getting down to the archives," said a now-rather-pert Mary-Elizabeth. "I said to the people when I went onto the board that I had not got many qualifications for being on the Trust governing body, but I could be the unpaid archivist because I'd put the records together in the first place. I'd just continue with the work, dividing it into subject matters, putting the papers in chronological order and so on. Felicity is helping me out—the academic brain, you know."

"Oh, yes, of course. Well, you mustn't let me . . . I'm sure Stafford will be delighted that you're doing this. He's been saying ever since we moved into the house that it needed attention, but every moment of his day gets used up by the house and rooms and the Great War exhibition. . . . So on his behalf I'll say thank you. We're so grateful. I'll leave you to get on with it."

She backed out of the little cubbyhole, where she had been standing too close to the pair for comfort. Her footsteps were heard again, this time going downstairs. The pair looked at each other.

"Not her usual rather grand self," said Felicity.

"By no means. I'm usually in awe of her, but today she seemed rather fearful of us."

"I must be getting along."

"Oh, by the way, before you slip off: what was the date of the letter you read out to me? About the cycle thing."

Felicity picked up the carbon copy. "Oh, it's August . . . August 1939."

They looked at each other, both of them frowning.

CHAPTER 8

Past History

✳

"Well, young feller me lad, you seem to have three hands full."

Charlie had not been called a feller me lad since he was in single figures, but he rather liked it, and the man who used this dated cheeriness. Rupert Fiennes had from the first struck him as an utterly genuine man, with a strong vein of mercy in the judgments he made— Charlie got this view from Felicity, who had by now had several chats with him. Of course Charlie reserved judgments, in the way that policemen were bound to, but he was impressed that Felicity felt she could assure him that Rupert bore no malice against Sir Stafford, nor did he seem to feel that the family was divided into hostile wings that needed to work against each other as a matter of principle and in the family tradition. Charlie hitched his one-year-old-at-a-pinch farther up on his shoulder.

"I do, don't I? I imagined the second child was going to be easier than the first, but it doesn't work out like that, does it? Thomas is an angelic kid, but still . . ."

"I get your point, though I've no experience," said Rupert. "Any chance of us having coffee together, or something stronger, at some other time if not now?"

"Sure. I must say *now* sounds rather inviting. Carola, Thomas, you'd like an orange or something, wouldn't you?"

"Yes," chorused both children, Carola supplying comments for Thomas. She put up her hand to be led to the watering hole.

When they had adopted a table in the saloon bar of Halifax's White Heifer and Carola was going in and out to the play area under the eye of a benevolent barmaid, Rupert came back with two pints of Landlord's and set them down at the table. Nobody mentioned coffee again. When Rupert Fiennes sat back in his chair, pulled out his pipe, and put it on the table as a sort of protest, Charlie felt he had suddenly been adopted and become a part of an England that had nearly vanished.

"Landlord's," he said. "Couldn't be better. You must want something out of me."

"Not at all," said Rupert Fiennes, stroking his mustache. "I thought you might want something out of me. Your wife is obviously very interested in the past of the house I once called home, and it occurred to me that I might find it easier to talk to you, tell you what I remember about things in the past—or at least tell you what I've been told. Until the 1930s the house had very little to interest anyone in its past or its present. Later on . . . Well, as I say, Felicity has been asking questions, and there's every reason why she should. It's part of her job, as a board member."

"So you'd like to put your side of this past?" said Charlie cheekily.

"There is no side," said Rupert, smiling comfortably. "I hated living in Walbrook and eventually got out. Stafford loved and still loves it. Far from bearing him malice, I'm enormously grateful, and I acknowledge my luck: I was keen to get rid of Walbrook, and there was Stafford waiting and eager, like an elderly puppy."

"Not exactly to buy you out, though."

"But I'd settled for any solution other than that years ago. There was no acceptable way of selling Walbrook as it was. Stafford was the ideal solution."

"So in a way—" Charlie stopped, wondering how to put this. "Though Stafford's only chairman of the board, and he's only chair as long as his board wants him to be, yet in a way he has taken over the old roles of his wing of the family, the roles they had lost in—was it 1939?"

"Yes." Rupert's voice took on Churchillian overtones. "A fateful year, and I was not yet alive to give it even a baby's attention. Stafford was, though. He was about three or four when war broke out, and—in his babyish way—he knew Walbrook, and especially the Dower House. He had lived there while his mother went for treatment to the Leeds General Infirmary."

"Ah, yes," said Charlie, not wanting to cross that bridge and ruin the atmosphere. "We'd wondered about that. But we're getting ahead of ourselves if the reason the house changed hands was a financial crisis in the Quarles wing of the family."

Rupert nodded and stroked his pipe. "Yes, we are. That

was the reason, though there were complicating factors. The pressures on the landed gentry went back to the nineteenth century, so they had been getting poorer and poorer over a long period, and the slaughter in the First World War had left many families like ours impoverished of talent or a nose for money. Timothy did his best, I'm sure, when he inherited the place from his father in 1921, but he wasn't the son his father would have chosen, and his best wasn't nearly good enough. He knew very little of how to run a place like Walbrook Manor, nor how to get money out of it. He was at sea, and he knew it."

"Who was it who suggested the weekend seminars on peace?"

"Nobody knows, but some of us suspect it was a man called Maurice Matlock, minor—very—composer, interferer in any artistic project going, general busybody, and one fascinated by the politics of the right-wing movements in Europe—Mussolini in Italy, Salazar in Portugal, later Hitler, Franco, and all sorts of gray and dubious figures in Eastern Europe. More of him later. Timothy may have thought up the peace seminars himself or had them suggested by a stranger in a pub, but Maurice Matlock is a prime candidate because he was a born mover and shaker behind the scenes—rather like Lord Mandelson today."

"But Timothy lived long enough after the sale to tell *some*one the tale, didn't he?"

"It would have been a sanitized version. My father threatened him: if he tried to misrepresent those seminars as purely pacifist in aim and tone, he would make public the truth."

"Which was?"

"That over the years they had become a front movement for the fascist forces that were sweeping over Europe."

"Guaranteed, if there was evidence, to blacken any attempt to whitewash the past?"

"Absolutely. After 1939, everyone involved was careful to forget those fabulous weekends at Walbrook. And of course the peace movement did begin as a legitimate cause: this—anything like the slaughter of the Great War—must never happen again. An understandable and legitimate cause. A lot of the activity sprang from that feeling, and one would use the word *well-meaning* of the whole movement if the word had not become rather suspect. Artists and intellectuals were attracted to the cause in great numbers."

"People like the composers who contributed to the song cycle?"

"Exactly. We think the man who had the idea for the cycle was Ivor Gurney, minor poet and composer, one of the many fighters in the trenches who lost not his life but his sanity there—his *balance* is perhaps the best way of putting it. He suggested the song cycle, we think, to Maurice Matlock, and the thing took off from there. Gurney was in an asylum, so he could not really drum up contributors. The job went to Matlock, and he did a superb job. He got a whole list of names from the older generation of composers—Bax, Vaughan Williams, Elgar—and as the thirties' drift to war gathered pace, the younger generation as well: Walton, Britten, Tippett. I'm talking about agreements to take part, not actual music written. That was much more difficult to bring about. These were the middle-aged and current generations of English music. They had to be left alone with their inspiration. That was why very little had been finalized by the time Gurney died in 1937. Matlock took the enterprise over entirely after that, tried to make the project into something practical and concrete, something that would soon be ready for performance, but it never came to that."

Charlie shook his head. "I begin to see. It may be a red herring. The main thing was that for the moment the financial state of the family and house were improved. Except that by 1939 the policy of appeasement was a busted flush and everyone was prepared for—mentally, I mean—the war that came in September."

"That's right. No more peace seminars then."

"And is this when your father entered the picture?"

Rupert grinned. "I'd say he pushed himself into it, rather than just entered. He was a determined man, who thought in terms of simple moral choices. He had always been suspicious of pacifists, as most middle- or upper-class people were at the time. Gradually he became aware of what was going on at Walbrook, and he was livid with rage. Where Timothy Quarles thought the slaughtered millions of young men in the First war had earned a better fate for the next generation, my dad, Montague Fiennes, thought they deserved beatification: their cause was still my dad's. He was already very suspicious of the Quarles branch, due to something that happened in 1790 or thereabouts—a dubious legitimacy I seem to remember. He was ready by 1938 to try to take over the house."

"How? Was your father rich? What did he do?"

"He was owner and managing director of a chain of hotels. His genes must have inherited the family's founder's genes. We were very nicely off is probably the best way of putting it. He was still a youngish man in 1938, with a glamorous second wife. I wasn't born until 1946. He went along to Walbrook and put it to Timothy, and Tim laughed in his face. Ten years before he might have accepted, my father was told, but now the financial stability of house and family were looking rosy. 'No thank you very much' was the essence of what was said. He added, 'And don't come back.'"

"But your father did?"

"Oh, he did—dramatically. In the train going back to London, he read the headline of the paper he'd bought at the station: 'Hitler's unalterable decision on Czechoslovakia.' He got out at the next station and took the train back to Halifax. He burst in on Timothy, pointed out that the situation was completely changed, and his offer was reduced by three thousand pounds."

"Doesn't sound much," said Charlie.

"At that time, and talking of stately homes, it was a lot."

"So, a determined man," judged Charlie. "Unforgiving."

"Yes. I don't know where all that determination went when I was made," said Rupert. "I won't give you all the ins and outs but by the summer of the next year Timothy was convinced of what was staring him in the face: if he didn't sell up to his second cousin, his name and the seminars he hosted would be blacker than oily mud. He sold up, bought an unwanted vicarage in Essex, and that was the last Dad saw of him, though there were some acrimonious contacts by post."

"And your father took over as Lord High Everything else at Walbrook?"

"Not quite. He knew that in wartime he could not hope to run a hotel chain and even a modest-sized gentry residence. He offered the house at a peppercorn rent to the government as a home for those with mental troubles—living in the community was not an option back then. They jumped at the idea, and Dad in one fell swoop established the Fienneses' patriotic commitment of family and home in wartime. No one brought up the peace seminars, and the new dispensation was even welcomed in the village. Dad was no Croesus, but he was more generous than your average country gentleman with a financial problem that was near insoluble."

"Then at the end of the war," said Charlie, "your dad took the house back?"

"That's right. Nineteen forty-seven it was. Dad was lord of the manor, in his own eyes at least. The title doesn't exist in fact, but people could flatter him by using it."

"You came into the world."

"I was just a baby when we moved. Symbolic, at least in intention. In fact the family finances were stretched, as Timothy's had been, though the house was run much more efficiently, as you'd expect. While I was growing up, there was a bit of 'One day, Son, all this will be yours.' But I never really felt it or wanted it. It didn't feel like mine, didn't feel like a home, though maybe it did to Mary-Elizabeth."

"Your attitude must have been a blow to your dad."

"Oh, I never told him. He was pleased enough when I went into the army, and he just assumed that when he died, I would buy myself out of the army and take over. He had all sorts of things to occupy his mind. In the sixties he got rid of the hotels, then he worked for the Conservative Party in the Halifax area—a hard-pressed bunch. He had the knighthood but he was promised a life peerage in the early eighties; the coming of Margaret Thatcher got him all excited, and so did the fact that I was ingloriously employed in the Falklands invasion, which he thought was appropriate. He was just thinking over what to call himself—Lord Fiennes of Walbrook I'd guess—when he dropped down dead. Collapse of stout party."

"You don't sound as if you were heartbroken."

"Oh, I was fond of the old boy. But I was sickened by the Falklands affair and all the bogus flag-waving it involved. Before the Argentineans invaded, Thatcher begrudged the islanders a supply ship once a year. I tossed up and it came down that I'd leave the army and take over Walbrook. I don't regret it, not at all, but still . . ."

"But still what?"

"It was never my sort of house. Like most military men I like a Spartan existence—the basic essentials, but not too much padding. But I was never made to be a gentleman, a landlord, a recipient of unearned income. It's been a long, hard haul."

"And you had your cousin as an added burden on your income."

"Oh, Mary-Elizabeth. She's been around pretty much all my life. Almost a sister to me. She's been company for me, adviser, the real lord, or lady, of the manor, and then everything else as well. I don't think of her as a burden at all."

"And yet finally you got rid of the place."

"Yes, and heartily glad I've been to rid myself of it. Mary-Elizabeth will be glad too, when she realizes how much easier and pleasanter life is. We've got the upstairs flat in what used to be the doctor's house in the village. We have to go to Halifax for our doctoring. It's not ideal, but most people in the village have a car. There's still a bus service, which there wouldn't be if this was in the South of England—yes, life is much sweeter."

"And Sir Stafford?"

"What about Sir Stafford?"

"Do you get on?"

"To be sure we do. As much as is necessary."

"You think he's straight?"

Rupert Fiennes rubbed his chin. "Oh, dear—does the notion of straightness still survive? I don't meet up with many straight people in my daily life. Even in the army it's a dead concept. Look at the people in Iraq and Afghanistan. The service chiefs are always stabbing each other in the back. Then the three of them get together to do the politicians down. To listen to them speak, you'd think that all the wartime leaders before them had only to request men, machines, and equipment and it was bought and put at their disposal. Cloud cuckoo land, but people believe it, and so do newspaper editors—what a stupid lot *they* are! Sir Stafford, I'd say, is as straight as most people today."

"And you'll go on working with him?"

"I suppose so. If I get fed up with it, and him, I can easily get out from under."

"Is there anything upsetting you?"

Rupert's chin was fingered again. "I suspect Sir Stafford has set up a board that is broadly well-informed, impressive-looking. But I think he will dispense with the services of anyone who disagrees with him or looks likely to disagree with him. Like most people he prefers to act with puppets rather than with potential rivals."

"And how are you going to respond to a development like that—a takeover, I mean? Would you fight it?"

"Not on your life! I've done more than enough fighting in my life, and rather incompetently. Like I say, I'd get out from under."

"Why? Because you don't really like the house?"

"I like the house all right. I just don't want to live in it. And why should I oppose Sir Stafford making it a one-man show? He loves the house, he's a museum expert, he gets on—moderately—well with people. He's not going to live forever, and he's not going to do anything monstrous or inappropriate to the house. I'd hand it to him on a plate."

"And the royalties and performance fees from *From the Trenches* or whatever the song cycle comes to be called—would you hand them to him?"

"No, of course not. This is part of the contents of the house that were handed over to the Trust. Stafford can't touch it. If I'm interpreting the messages right, the receipts won't be enormous. What you've got are good English composers going through their paces. Not exactly on an off day, but not really at their best. A few performances, maybe a recording, and then consigned to the bottom drawer. I think even Matlock realized that."

"Tell me about Matlock."

"I think I saw him when I was a child, but I don't remember anything about it. There are some photographs, so they are my substitutes for memory. He looks repellent."

"In what way? Smarmy?"

"Yes. Or maybe *oily* describes it better. Periodically over the years he came to Walbrook, apparently to check a music manuscript, really to chart whether any unknown manuscripts had been found that were intended for the song cycle. He was almost entirely in charge of that project by then, but very little progress seemed to be made toward either publication or performance. One of my favorite pictures of him was taken at the end of one such visit. It just shows his back."

"And?" asked Charlie, curious.

"He had just left the house and was going down the hill to his car. My father was watching him from the bedrooms. Matlock forgot that he could still be seen from the house, and after a time he broke into a dance—'a sort of joyful polka,' my father said—and you can see the dance from the photograph: his feet hardly seem to be touching the ground."

"What do you think he was celebrating? Did your father know?"

"He didn't, but he was determined to find out. He had been suspicious for a long time—hence the camera. He rang the local police super, who in turn rang his opposite number in Camden, where the oily Matlock lived. They were waiting for him when he got home and found it in his luggage."

"What was it?"

"It was another song for the cycle. He said he must have made a mistake when he was putting his things away in his briefcase. They took that with a pinch of salt, but this was white-collar crime if it was a crime at all, and the bobbies in London didn't feel at home with it. They let him off with a caution and returned the music to my father. He was not well—it was shortly before his death—and he didn't want to be troubled by anything involving Matlock. So that was the end of it. As Dad said, wryly, it was a very short song."

"You must have taken over shortly afterward."

"That's right. Nineteen eighty-three. I was one of several young men discontented in the army. Mary-Elizabeth ran things briefly till I could get my release, and then we started on a regime of economizing, making do, retrenching. It was quite satisfying for a while, but eventually we had to face the fact that it wouldn't work. In spite of Mary's enthusiasm for cutting our coat according to our cloth, we faced an old age of living in a house that was becoming a ruin around us."

"A pretty grim prospect," agreed Charlie.

"I'm in love with our flat. Everything works, and everything is simple and efficient. I'm learning to cook—all the basics and some quite difficult recipes. I watch all the would-be chefs on daytime television. Heaven! So don't tell me I could make trouble for Stafford. He's got carte blanche as far as I'm concerned."

Charlie took a swig of his beer and thought.

"But you did want to talk with me, didn't you? Put your point of view."

"Yes. I face a future of standing round at wine-and-cheese parties in my old house and being pointed out as the last lord of the manor, the man who could never quite make ends meet. I just like to put my own angle on things now and then."

"I liked him," said Charlie that night over dinner. "Believed him too. Not that I'm lowering my defenses. I've known people who fifty years ago would have been hanged and yet they were just as believable as Rupert Fiennes. But still . . ."

"Is it possible for someone like that to be so lukewarm about families as he is?" asked Felicity.

"Of course it is. Look at yourself."

"I'm not gentry. And I do think about family. I wonder how my mother could have married my awful father and then stayed loyal to him through the whole of that marriage. And then there's my grandmother—I remember her as a sensible lady. Why didn't she stop her daughter making that dreadful mistake?"

"You don't stop children marrying these days."

"That wasn't these days."

"I don't care tuppence about family," said Charlie.

"My scatterbrained mother is mainly an embarrassment. My father I could pass in the street—in fact I could arrest him in the street—and not have the faintest idea he was my father. So could my mother."

"You never had childish fantasies about being the secret love child of a member of the royal family?"

"Me? The color I am? I've never had any doubt about my father being as black as my mother."

"Not caring much about family background seems to go hand in hand with parents not caring about their offspring. Let 'em do what they like. Let them do what they like, because eventually that's what they will do. So the parents don't fight drugs, or knives, or very early sex. And if they don't care, why should the children?"

"That's not my background, and my mother did try and had some success. Anyway, we're getting off the subject, which is that we have no case."

"We never had a case or expected to find one," Felicity pointed out. "I've just been intrigued by Walbrook and Sir Stafford and the family dynamics."

"Agreed. Sir Stafford, who was the starting point, turns out to be a typical committee member on an arts body—committed and knowledgeable, but with a strong vein of egotism underneath. He also has a personal interest in Walbrook. Beyond that, we've found that he probably would like to have a collection of yes-men and yes-women around him. Not necessarily a bad thing, and possibly a positive one: your own yes-men can make for a more united and effective board than one with many different egotisms pulling in different directions."

"Agreed. What it comes down to is, situation normal,

nothing worse than occasional personal disagreements, things on the whole going well with visitor figures, local PR, the special exhibition, and so on."

"Everything in the garden is lovely," said Charlie.

But of course that was before the discovery of the body.

CHAPTER 9

Wet Bones

*

The woman taking the path down to the pool known as Haroldswater (chivying her two young children and their dog along the path behind her and exclaiming at familiar natural phenomena) exuded moral authority, young as she was. At her place of work her attributed name was Trouble, as in "Here comes trouble," though others more favorably disposed attached to her the more cumbersome "the done thing." She was continually asking herself what the regulations said, and why they said it. When she had discovered that, she generally knew what the done thing was and followed her nose.

Once beside the water, her family's favorite place for an impromptu picnic, she opened the small basket, took from it a rather basic set of packages containing cheese sandwiches, biscuits, and fruitcake, and placated the children with a selection from each package. They all settled down, chattering happily, and occasionally feeding the dog, who was called Peggotty. Beside their picnicking place was a notice warning against swimming in Haroldswater, which in places had surprising depths. The woman did not need warning, and while she chattered and pointed out birds and even a fox on the other side of the water, she kept her eyes on her children with her ear taking in all the time the subjects of their chattering. When half the picnic was eaten, she packed the remainder away for later on, and they all went down to paddle in the shallowest and safest places, with Peggotty practicing her powers of self-advertisement. They paddled and splashed until the mother said it was time to eat up the food and start for home. She looked toward the shore and shook her head.

"Oh, dear. What's Peggotty got now?"

The dog was barking a "Haven't I been clever?" sort of bark, one she used often, and was standing over two white, solid objects that she had found somewhere or other and laid out neatly on the shore. The woman gained the earthy shore and was about to pick them up when she said, "Good heavens," and held herself back.

"What is it, Mummy?"

"I don't know. I think I have to get someone out here."

She pulled out her mobile phone and spoke into it, the children on either side of her in trained total silence.

"Kath? I need help. I need someone who knows what's what out here. It's Haroldswater—you know where it is, don't you? . . . I mean 'what's what' medically and criminally. I'm here with the children, and I won't go away till I've handed over to someone who is a detective policeman, not a boffin like me. . . . Hurry, Kath. The children are inclined to be boisterous, and I'd like to get them out of the crime scene, if there is one."

She slipped the phone into her jeans pocket.

"Mummy, Mummy—what is it? What did Peggotty find? Is this really a crime scene? Tell us."

"I think, darlings, that Peggotty discovered a human bone, and a separate finger bone. They're wet, and I guess they have been in the water a long time."

That human remains had been found by a member of the West Yorkshire forensics team, and a female one at that, was the cause of jokes and sexist badinage for the whole team at the Halifax station. Charlie did not participate. He had collected any detectives not obviously working on a case and taken them to Haroldswater. He had heard a lot about Dr. Julie Maddison, seen her once or twice, and thought she was someone with whom he could work, though he thought her Olympic-gymnast body was a little bit off-putting. When he found that, because of her part in the discovery, she was not professionally to have anything to do with her findings, he was part regretful, part delighted.

"I don't know this Haroldswater place," he said to her at Police Headquarters. "Is it near a churchyard? Could the bones have been separated from the rest of the body during flooding? We've had enough of floods in the last few years."

"The nearest graveyard is three miles away, and the pool is too high to have been hit by flooding," said Dr. Julie.

"Do you have a hunch about how long it has been dead?"

"Yes. And my hunch would be no better than your hunch."

"I doubt it. I only caught a glimpse of it out there. Go on—guess."

"My hunch is that it's been dead a long, long time."

"Anglo-Saxon? The age of Shakespeare? The body of Catherine Earnshaw?"

"No, no. Later than those."

"Well, go on: *about* when?"

She shook her head. "Charlie, shut up. You asked for a hunch, and now you're turning it into a professional scientific verdict. I'm not having any."

"Right. Look—I promise not to quote your guess to anyone. It's a bet between you and me with no money on it because you're guessing with say twenty years on either side, while I have all the rest of recorded time. Just a lovely private bet between the two of us—a secret à deux."

"You think you can charm the birds down from their branches. People told me that, and they were dead right. Well, here goes. Somewhere around the middle of the last century. Give it your twenty on either side and that makes it somewhere between 1930 and 1970. Got that? If it's wrong, I never said it, right? Now let me get on with my work."

Charlie wandered away, his brain ticking over but not making him shout *Eureka* at any point. The only breakthrough was when he saw PC Murray Weston snatching a quick lunch at his desk, the chutney oozing down his chin.

"Murray, you're from Walbrook, aren't you? What's

the name of the gaffer there who knows everyone that's ever lived there, and everything that's ever happened in the village since he was in toweling nappies back in the twenties?"

"Oh, you mean Jeb Wheeler. A human encyclopedia within a very narrow field."

"Is he still reasonably compos mentis?"

"Wrong tense. *Was* till he died? Yes, he was, but it didn't stop him dying."

That stopped Charlie. "Really? I felt sure . . . How long ago was this? Last week?"

"Last year, if not the year before. We miss him."

"Who does? Us here at the station?"

"Yes. We miss him, and we'd miss him even more if Walbrook was a hotbed of crime."

Charlie was frowning. "I just can't get over . . . Still, there must be someone else who may do—someone who really knows the village through and through. Who might that be?"

"I'd go after his son. You'll get it all at one remove, but he'll have all the stories pat. He'll have heard them oftener than anyone would like. And by the way, I wouldn't mind betting he'll have some that were not for general consumption. Interesting character, Will."

"Why's that?"

"He's been a gay proselytizer all his life. He's currently secretary of the Association of Rural Gays. In the past he's been something or other in the Society of Gay Athletes."

"A man of various lifestyles," said Charlie. "I have a feeling my wife has met him. I'll give her a ring later on."

As is the usual thing with cases involving bodies and bones, things piled up on Charlie's desk, as well as things involving him in travel and questioning, so it was after five when he actually rang Felicity on his mobile. She was home, coping with two demanding (in different ways) children.

"Hi, Charlie. I'm busy, but they're asking to talk to you."

"Later. You first. You told me about a guy in pink trousers, one of the dog walkers of Walbrook. Was his name Will?"

"No idea. They none of them told me their names. I just called them in my own mind Cockles, Paunch, Pink Trousers, and so on."

"So the name means nothing to you?"

"Nothing at all. His father had been head gardener at Walbrook."

"Yes, you told me that. What time was it you met this little group?"

"Late morning—say eleven or so."

"And did you get the impression that this was a regular occurrence in their day—the dog walking I mean? Did they meet up then to talk over last night's telly, discuss who should win *Britain's Got Talent* and so on?"

"Regular—yes. Topics of conversation—something less asinine, I'd guess. Might even be politics on a good day. Village life is real, and earnest, however they may cover that with a joking surface act."

"I'm told that the man I think must be Pink Trousers is a good person to ask about the village scandals of the last fifty or sixty years. Would you agree?"

"Maybe. He's—I would guess—only in his late middle-age."

"And you said he had a father—won't go into that now—employed at Walbrook in a role conducive to gossip and rumors. The police used him often."

"That'll suit you down to the ground. You've got a lot more on him than I did. I had the impression that the group of men—mostly older than Pink Trousers—was holding back on me, keeping quiet about any really juicy morsel. You could speak to all of them, but I would suspect you'd get more out of Pink Trousers, especially if you talk to him on his own."

So when he strolled over to the group of elderlies and no-longer-youngs the next morning, Charlie recognized some of them, which in the case of Pink Trousers did not take much brainwork.

"Hi," he said, "I'm the—"

"The policeman," said Paunch. "Your day is made, Will. He's come to rummage in your great mind."

"He can rummage anywhere he pleases," said Will. "Where shall we do this exciting catechism?"

"Yours please, not mine," suggested Charlie, and he was about to be led off, feeling like a prize pig, when Cockles put his spoke in.

"You connected to that nice bint who talked to us last week?"

"More than connected—married. We do things by the book in the police force."

"Not what I've heard," said Paunch.

"How did you know this?" Charlie asked Cockles.

"Oh, come on. She comes and works in the Big

House, she asks questions, most of the museum assistants are from the village. Put all that together and what do you get? Of *course* everyone knew she was married to a policeman. They could also see that he's black, not white. Really sharp, aren't we, us village folk?"

"Well, if you think there's something I ought to know that you have particular knowledge of, tell me. You can ring me at the Leeds police number."

"Right. 'Can I speak to Charlie Peace, please?' Is that the way to your ear?"

"Dexter Peace to the receptionist, though she knows I answer to Charlie. Come on, Mr. Wheeler."

On the walk to Wheeler's cottage they talked about dogs, and the impossibility of having one with a policeman's work schedule and two young children. The longer they talked, the more Will Wheeler's camp impersonations fell away, so that by the time he let them into a tiny but attractive cottage with clematis, not roses, around the door, they were talking quite normally.

The ground floor was a model of what can be done with very little space. The area was open, with kitchen and eating and relaxing space all together and apparently functioning well. The wall made the strongest personal-political statement, being plastered with male pinups: a few of them hunks, including figures from the Australian soaps, but most of them willowy, pretty young men, all of them totally unclothed. Charlie definitely felt he had been presented with a surfeit of penises.

"Not many blacks," he said cheerfully.

Will Wheeler grinned. "No offense, but they incline to

the beefy. I find beefiness comic rather than stimulating. Now—what can I do for you? I mean that in the chastest sense."

"Good. Tell me about Walbrook, and tell me the most controversial, the most dangerous, of your father's stories about the place. Pull no punches."

Will Wheeler thought before answering.

"The house or the village?"

"Both."

"As far as village gossip is concerned, it has always been ninety to ninety-five percent usual rural stuff: pregnant maidens, errant vicars, randy milkmen, even the odd camp character, like me, whom they had to take in their stride because they were afraid of my dad, a formidable figure. There was an interesting pregnancy, but maybe we could come back to that."

"Perfectly okay. You're in the driving seat on this. What about the manor? I've heard a lot about the pacifist seminars that turned out to be less than pacific."

"Right." Will sat massaging his knee, thinking about the time before he came into existence, as it had been rendered in his father's account. "The seminars and their attendees were the main village talking point in the thirties, when my dad was one of the gardeners up at the house. That went on until the house was sold, and by then a lot of the occasional celebrity visitors to the seminars had packed their bags and taken themselves off to the United States. Benjamin Britten, Peter Pears, Christopher Isherwood, and so on."

"How controversial were the seminars in Walbrook?"

"Oh, enormously," said Will, spreading his hands to

underline their enormity. "They were unpopular on two fronts, two reasons: first there were the pacifist aims that dominated all the publicity about the weekends. Even the mass slaughter in the First World War didn't affect the village statement of faith that if your country called you, you packed your kit bag and obeyed the summons to fight. But then there was the behavior of some of the attendees, not least the celebrities. Shocking, ducky! You wouldn't believe! Only everyone did, of course. The stories kept happy a population that television had not yet reached."

"Did the scandal involve Timothy Quarles?"

Will's face dropped. "Ah, you clearly know all about it already. My big moment is aborted."

"You mentioned an interesting pregnancy and I've heard that someone has mentioned an illegitimate child."

"Well, at least I can fill you in. It was a girl from the village, which made it worse, not better. She was a kitchen maid at Walbrook: that meant scrubbing and scraping and the rough laundry. Rose Patchett was about twenty, very stupid, but with an eye for the main chance, which she thought would be the making of her, though as far as we knew, it was the breaking."

"Did she try to get money out of Timothy?"

"Of course she did. Wouldn't you?"

"Maybe. But it was a dangerous course to take."

"Oh, yes. When I think how many weapons Timothy must have had, and how very few Rose had, then I wonder whether I'd have risked it. But I've a lot of the coward in me. Maybe I'd have said some village thickie

I'd slept with was the father and gratefully accepted a five-pound note from the lord of the manor."

"I see your point. So what happened to her?"

"Rumor had it she went to London."

"Nobody heard from her? Not her parents?"

"Not her parents, who were staunch Methodists. But Walbrook saw her once again. The village saw her when she drove through—yes, *drove*—with a baby in the passenger seat. The manor saw her ten minutes later. She went to the kitchen, the part of the house she knew best. One of the seminars was on, so everyone was up to their eyes in work, but they took time off for a cup of tea. Her driving a car was the principal cause of comment. They couldn't believe she could get a driving license, recently brought in. They were right. Rose said she 'wasn't bothered' by such things. When asked why she was there, she said 'to make arrangements' about the baby—no one asked his or her sex. Seeing herself losing her audience, she snatched the baby and ran from 'belowstairs' up to the main rooms of the house. And that was the last time she was seen in Walbrook. No one saw her drive off. Mourned by no one, and only useful as the subject of gossip."

"Such as?"

"Someone said he'd seen her in the Mall on VE Day, but he later admitted it could have been anyone. Just a vague resemblance that could have been the dress she and a million other girls had bought with their clothing coupons. If she set up as a whore, none of the squaddies from the village would have admitted using her. End of Rose. She was no great loss to village life."

"No. And the loss included the baby, presumably."
Charlie was very hot on neglected babies.

"Never seen again. Disposed of some way or other."

"In both cases disposal could have involved murder."

"Sure. I don't see murder as a very Walbrook thing,
but I'm a strong union man, and I believe the gentry and
the aristocracy are capable of anything."

"You think that Timothy could have killed her, or had
her killed?"

Will spread out his hands, a familiar gesture of having
nothing to offer. "To tell you the truth, I don't 'think'
anything. It's a long time ago and I can't see any point
in reviving the matter." The moment the words were out
of his mouth, he put his hand over it. "Oh! The bones in
Haroldswater!"

Charlie raised his eyebrows theatrically. "So you know
about the bones. . . . When exactly was this scandal?"

"Exactly I don't know. Before my time. Say midthir-
ties. Maybe when the old king died, 1936 or so—you
wouldn't be far wrong."

"And the car was never found?"

"Nobody so far as we knew claimed it, so we assumed
nobody found it. The assumption was—assumption by
those like my dad who lived through the whole affair—
that she had been to see Timothy and afterward she
drove away into obscurity. If she'd had a car accident,
and the car had been found, the police would have con-
tacted her parents. They remained untroubled by their
un-Methodistical daughter."

"It's all very interesting," said Charlie truthfully. "Its
relevance to what I'm investigating I'm not sure about."

He remembered Felicity's conviction that the dog-walking men were keeping something from her. "Unless Rose's story figured in the negotiations between Mr. Quarles and Mr. Fiennes. Something on the personal level to run parallel with something on the political level."

"If it didn't figure in the haggling, it should have done," said Will, the union man.

"What exactly do you mean?"

"The haggling took place up to September 1939. The last days of peace, the first of war. Old Man Fiennes should have realized that the days of the landed gentry were numbered. He had money, infinitely more than the Quarles, but he should have asked himself, did he have enough?"

"To take on the burden of Walbrook?"

"Yes. To take on the burden of a decaying house two and a half centuries old. Old Fiennes found it was like funding the drugs bills of a hypochondriac. Every month there was something crumbling, something failing to function. He really took it on not in 1939 but in 1947, when the local council closed it as an asylum. They couldn't get out fast enough, and that should have wised him up. Hotel chains hadn't exactly made money in the war and its aftermath, and they would have needed to make mints of it. He found himself lumbered with this gentry residence with no money coming in to run it, a government hostile to landowners, and constant calls on his time, patience, money—you name it, he had too little of it. He relied on his young son to take over after him, and he never realized it would be the last thing Rupert wanted. I called him Old Man Fiennes a moment ago. He wasn't an old man when he bought Walbrook, but he was long before he died."

"Was Rupert married?"

"Had been. They'd been separated. She's still alive, I believe, but there's no communication between the two."

"Mark her off the list," said Charlie cheerfully.

"Oh, do you have a list?" said Will, obviously delighted. *"Cherchez la femme disparue?"*

"No, but I will have one before very long."

And his list, headed by Rose Patchett, received a new entry more quickly than he had bargained for. He was tracing his way along the paths he had taken with Will Wheeler earlier that morning when he was conscious, as soon as he entered the manor's grounds, of somebody targeting him. The dog scampering round his heels was a boarder terrier, and this, as well as the man's square shape and brisk, no-nonsense swagger, identified him as the one Felicity had called in her mind Cockles.

"I've a message for you," the man shouted. "From Will."

Charlie frowned, then twigged that Will had had an idea since Charlie had left his idyllic cottage. "Oh, yes, mobile phones. I shouldn't assume that Yorkshire villages haven't yet caught up with the infernal things."

"Practically every household has one," agreed Cockles. "Invaluable for ordering takeaway suppers. Will says will you put on your list, if you haven't already done so, the director's wife, Delia Gannett."

"I know whose wife she is. But she's dead, and everybody knows that."

Cockles shook his balding head. "Will says, 'She's no longer with us, and everyone's been told she's dead.' Quite a big difference there. Come on, Vini."

Cockles strode off toward the stable block, leaving Charlie with the idea that he was going to land up with a surfeit of missing ladies. Curiouser and curiouser.

CHAPTER 10

Onlookers

*

The next day was a Tuesday. For reasons that Felicity was unable to fathom, attendance at Walbrook Manor on a Tuesday was always meager, and there was talk about making Tuesday a closed day, when cleaning and minor repairs could take place. Ideal, Felicity thought. When she had taken Carola to school and parked Thomas in his nursery, she took the road to Walbrook, waved her hand cheerily at the dog walkers, and marched into the house "as if she owned it," she told herself. She wondered whether she was getting the disease that too often afflicted trustees of large and beautiful properties.

"Hello, Susan," she said, slowing her pace and lingering around the ticket office, the usual inhabitant of which little box was by now something of a friend. "You're a bit lonely, aren't you? Tuesday blues is it?"

"Oh, you know by now we use Tuesdays for dusting and scrubbing, hurrying away if there are any visitors coming through. We may soon have it as a closed day, and that will make a lot of sense."

"I should think so," said Felicity, nodding. "People expect a house like this to be sparkling clean—no dust, no dirt, no marks on the linen—that's how people like to see the house—women anyway. If Charlie's anything to go by, men just don't notice."

"That's right," said Susan. "We need a woman's hand here. Lady Quarles isn't involved at that level, and no disrespect to Mr. Gannett, but there are things he wouldn't notice in a thousand years."

"I'm sure he does his best," said Felicity, thinking she had become a walking platitude in her new position. She added, "He misses his wife, I expect."

"He must do, and not just in the obvious ways. A woman's touch is unmistakable, and it's missing now."

"What was she like, his wife?"

"Oh, lovely!" The subject was obviously one for enthusiasm, even rapture. "A lady, and not to seem snobbish, that's what she was. She was delicate, refined, exquisite. You know if she did something, if she pronounced on something, she would get it absolutely right. I'm sure Wes noticed, if he didn't register, what a difference she made."

"How did they meet? Here, or in Australia?"

"Oh, in Australia. Delia had gone out to see one or two family members who had settled there. She loved the country, and she might well have remained there, at least for a while, if she hadn't met Wes."

"That seems the wrong way round."

"Ah, but you see Wes had never done the Australian

thing of going back 'home,' looking up roots, tracing a family tree. So when they got together, they thought, good, long trip to England should be the first thing they would do, *then* they should make the decision of which country they should try to settle in. You know Wes had been curator of a museum of sport."

"No, I didn't know."

"In Brisbane, I think. People have commented of course: wrong sort of background for this job. But he is so careful and painstaking that the snide remarks have tailed off."

"Good," said Felicity. "I'm a great believer in learning on the job."

"That's right. Wes always says, 'The principles are the same.' Anyway, they married in Australia, blued their savings on airfares and holidays, and before long he was back doing museum work and doing it well."

"How did he get jobs? Competition must be fierce these days in museums as well as everywhere else."

"He jokes and says, 'The Australian Mafia.' But I think it was probably her family. She was a Bowes-Cartwright."

Felicity blinked. "Doesn't mean anything to me."

"Nor to me," confessed Susan. "But it always impresses people who *do* know about families, and it *sounds* good—almost royal!" She heard the door open and whispered, "When she became pregnant, we treated it like she was producing an heir to the throne!"

Two middle-aged people silently proffered the right money, then without a smile took their tickets and their one-page house guide into the large Drawing Room.

"She was pregnant, was she?" whispered Felicity.

"Yes. Wes told head museum assistant Marge Beckwith—he made a bad mistake there. He told her it should go no further, and that made sure it would go right through the museum's staff. Not like Wes to be indiscreet, but I suppose he was so full of the news and so pleased and proud."

"Did she die in childbirth?"

"No, she didn't. She went to see one of the Leeds specialists because of some unusual pains, and he slapped her straight into hospital and, after a few days, sent her down to another specialist in London. Wes came back looking really shattered. 'It's not for the baby now,' he told Marge. 'It's Delia we've got to think of now.' Two months later she was dead."

"What of?"

"Lung cancer."

"Was she a heavy smoker?"

"Didn't smoke at all. Nonsmokers can get it, you know."

"I know. . . . Whenever he talks about her, you get the impression that he's broken—haunted still. Like having been dealt a hefty blow."

"You should have seen him just after it happened. He was inconsolable. 'I feel like killing myself,' he said over and over. Or, 'There's no point in it anymore.' He meant life, you see. He's quite a lot better now, though not the old Wes he was when he came. It was as much as Sir Stafford could do to get him to go to the funeral."

"Wasn't she buried here?"

"Oh, no," said Susan, who by now was rather enjoying herself, Felicity thought. "She was buried in one of those tiny West Country places with slightly comic names. He showed us pictures of the funeral. I think he was glad after all that he went. He said, 'It's made a closure,' though most of us feel he's very far from closure even now. We mother him. All the museum assistants are women, so we sort of compete in the mothering stakes. We would have shook our heads and carried on if it had happened to Annabel Sowerby, the first director. But then she was a woman, and I'm afraid she was nothing to us."

"She was sacked, wasn't she?"

"As near as. She was an epitome of efficiency—the wrong sort of efficiency that has to get things done—something, anything, an accomplishment to quote in the annual report and pat ourselves on the back for."

"What sort of thing was that?"

"Her idée fixe was the catalog. She was determined that everything that came with the transfer of Walbrook to the Trust should be cataloged. Sounds sensible enough. But we had no library- or museum-trained people on the staff then. That didn't stop her though. She and two assistants just charged in and did what they could in double-quick time. Sir Stafford said we had to follow scholarly good practice, absolutely and completely. It had to be, otherwise the whole procedure was ludicrous and useless. And that's what it turned out to be. With untrained staff the cataloging was inconsistent and more confusing than helpful. So she had to go. She was one of these one-idea people, and it just wasn't good enough."

Felicity had much to think about when she took her break from inspecting estate records. She walked out into estate sunshine, ate her sandwiches outside the cafeteria, and threw backward and forward in her mind an idea about the first director of Walbrook. It was interesting that when Annabel Sowerby came to Walbrook she saw her mission as protecting the collection (pictures, furniture, letters, accounts) from pillaging. She had to catalog all that was handed over by Rupert Fiennes to the Walbrook Trust: items that told the history of the house, its inhabitants, the area of West Yorkshire in which the house had been built, the historical backgrounds of the county as a whole. Felicity got up and left the greaseproof paper in one of the waste bins in the little garden. Then she began to walk around the house, relishing sun and breeze.

Did the predecessor of Wes Gannett suspect that items had gone missing before she had been appointed, and was she working against the clock to minimize the risk of further peculation? That left a whole lot of people under suspicion. But the main candidates would surely be Sir Stafford Quarles and his lady wife.

Felicity turned onto the hilly lawn on the north side of the manor. A path led down to the village. She had not taken much notice of this part of the estate before. She took notice now, though. The nearest house, in the village rather than the estate, was a handsome, Victorian, three-floor building, much too fine, she thought, to house Pink Trousers or any of the other village dog owners. The reason she wondered who lived there was that Charlie's car was parked in the drive of the house.

Charlie and Sergeant Hargreaves had arrived by appointment at two o'clock at the onetime Dower House of the estate. The slim but capable-looking girl who opened the door introduced herself as Mr. Quarles's nurse, and she led them through to the sunny, airy sitting room. The focal point of the room was a table, with on one side an upright chair and on the other an invalid chair. Most of the rest of the room was empty.

The man sitting in the invalid chair had his neck twisted and thrown back so that he seemed to be gazing intently at a picture rail. His mouth was slightly open, and in his "Good day" Charlie could distinguish no consonants. Perhaps he was saving them for more than conversational courtesies.

"It's Mr. Peace from the police," said his nurse, making it sound like Gilbert and Sullivan. "With DS Hargreaves."

She was bringing in a chair for Hargreaves, whose presence was an optional extra.

"And this is . . . ?" said Charlie, for form's sake.

"This is Graham Quarles, brother of Sir Stafford Quarles."

"And a well-known composer," said Charlie, not holding out his hand because there would have been difficulties. "And you are . . . ?"

"I'm Lesley Soames. I'm the nurse and the amanuensis, but today I may have to act as interpreter as well."

"I'd be grateful if you would," said Charlie. "How long have you lived here, sir?"

Graham Quarles gestured toward his attendant with a single finger.

"He has lived here three years," she said, speaking distinctly so she could be corrected if necessary. "This was part of the agreement with the new Trust. Mr. Rupert was very insistent on that."

Charlie, as he went on, realized that Graham left answering to his attendant when simple matters of fact were raised. Who was he, Charlie Peace, to insist on normal procedures when his sergeant was concealing a tiny tape recorder about his burly person? Charlie took Lesley through Graham's shortened curriculum vitae: minor public school, a state scholarship to the Northern College of Music, a place in the BBC Symphony Orchestra, then the compositions that enabled him eventually (about 1989, said Lesley) to write music full-time. His stroke took place in the year 2002, and since then he had been an invalid, only able to compose because Lesley could act as his musical amanuensis.

"Marriage?" queried Charlie.

"No," said Lesley.

"Any long-lasting affair—or, let's say, partnership?"

Graham gestured to Lesley to keep quiet. This time Charlie heard a few consonants, but he was still reliant on Lesley for her sharpness as a translator.

"Mr. Quarles says there was one when he was in his twenties—"

Graham Quarles interrupted her, and she immediately translated.

"There was one with Betty Bartlett, a soprano now dead, and the other one"—she looked inquiringly at Graham—"was with Pia Corelli, an Italian cellist, and that was when he was in his forties."

"I see," said Charlie. "Is the lady still alive?"

There were grunts from the wheelchair.

"As far as he knows, and he doesn't care an iota one way or the other."

"Thank you. So this house serving as a retirement home for you was—what?—the brainchild of Sir Stafford?"

Graham took over answering, Lesley still translating.

"He says that as far as he knows, it was Rupert Fiennes who had the idea. Rupert has some remnants of the attitude that people call noblesse oblige. Of course when the suggestion was made, Sir Stafford was delighted to go along with it."

"And you are still able to compose music?"

"He says, very generously, that he is, with the help of me," said Lesley. "And he has strong support, financial support, from the Musicians' Benevolent Society."

"I see. Have you lived round here all your life, sir?"

Graham gestured again toward Lesley.

"Not at all," Lesley said briskly. "He lived in London when he had his orchestral job. That was necessary. He did a few years teaching at his old college in Manchester. Naturally his stroke caused problems. When the offer of Oakdene—that's this house—came, he was living in Leeds, and I went to his flat to help with his music two days a week. Now I'm a full-time maid of all work, and that suits us both very well."

"Do you manage to get around much?"

"He tries to get to first performances of his music. Mostly we succeed, with a bit of help. Mr. Wainwright, whom I've seen you talking to within the manor grounds, has been enormously helpful."

Cockles, thought Charlie, trying to picture chronologically the life that had been presented to him by Graham Quarles's nurse.

"Just to get this straight, sir: in the story I've heard, all the connections with Walbrook have come after the time when Mr. Quarles had his stroke." Charlie saw Graham Quarles frown, then smooth out his forehead. "Am I right in thinking there were no connections in your earlier life with either Walbrook or the Fiennes branch of the family?"

The strange sounds of Graham Quarles talking began almost at once.

"Almost right, but not quite," translated Lesley Soames. "I was here as a boy with my family. I remember nothing about it. This was when everyone was preparing for war. Soon there was the 'phony' war, then the Blitz, and so on. I was much too young to understand. The house was sold to the Fienneses; we were living in an old barn of a house in, or near, Witham in Essex. No connection between the two branches of the family, so far as I know, apart from business letters."

"And is that all?" asked Charlie.

"Not quite. When I was a young musician-cum-composer, I had a letter from the 'head of the family'—Rupert's father. There had been some publicity about me, I was 'making a name'—publicizing the Quarles name in fact."

"When was this?"

Quarles thought.

"About the midsixties. The letter asked me to lunch at the Salisbury Club. I was curious. I was half-starved. I decided to go. The food was dire, the decoration of the place drear beyond belief. It was as if the twentieth century had never battered its way in. Nothing but pictures of Tory notables over the last two centuries. It was a disastrous lunch. I was aggressive, he was condescending beyond belief. He knew nothing about music, but that didn't stop him talking nonsense about it. When we said good-bye outside the funereal dump, he said, 'We must do this again some time,' and I replied, 'Not on your life,' and walked off as quickly and finally as I could."

"You never saw him again?"

"No, not even by accident. He certainly never came to a concert where I was performing, or being performed."

"But you must have had dealings with Rupert and Mary-Elizabeth Fiennes."

"Ah, yes. Different kettle of fish, each in his own way. Rupert I could like, without wanting too much of his company."

"Why not?"

"Too limited. Typical soldier. You see why soldiers going into politics never really works. He's well-meaning—more than most military men—but he doesn't really *work* outside his own little sphere."

"And Mary-Elizabeth?"

"We've had less to do with her, though Lesley has enjoyed several chats with her, and so she has come into contact with her family feelings. Rather ridiculous, because the family, all the branches of it, has never really done very much. You know how with most people in Britain everything always comes back to class. You no sooner meet someone new and you start telling off the things in him and her which reveal their class: accent— very important—clothes, makeup in women, and so on. Most countries don't have this obsession, but we still do, and Mary-Elizabeth typifies this. Everything comes back to it, and her history of the family will be soaked in it."

This was the first time that Charlie had heard of anything so formal as a written history.

"And yet she is basically a poor relation, isn't she?"

"Oh, yes. The villagers say that when he took her in, old Fiennes, Rupert's dad, treated her as a sort of housemaid, or a bit later like the deputy manager of one of his prestigious hotels. Rupert thought this was nonsense, though the domestic part of her daily work became more and more important as the financial situation became more and more desperate. But she still judges everything by the old, stupid criteria: where he went to school, whether she went to finishing school. Absolutely daft, and pathetic as well. It's an obsession, so she'll suppress anything that conflicts with her ideas of the family's status."

"Suppress? What do you mean?"

"Tampering with the evidence. Nothing really serious, but it shows you what sort of a person she is. Take these so-called prewar seminars that you've probably heard about, with pacifist credentials apparently, but really stamping grounds for the European dictators, especially the worst of them, Adolf Hitler. When—if ever—her history is written, she'll include nothing whatever about the fascist dictatorships and the apologies for them that formed much of the meat of the seminars. And you can be pretty sure my good brother, Stafford, will not rush up with the evidence and say, 'You must deal with this.' Stafford has his own little games he seems to be playing. He's been good to me, so I'm not saying too much about it, but Stafford has his motives for everything."

"Meaning what? What is he suppressing and why?"

"Can't say, dear boy. But if I were you, I'd latch onto anything that seems to have gone missing. Songs from the song cycle that was sung here in December, for instance. Anyone who was anyone in the musical world in the thirties was asked to submit a song for consideration. All the ones that are left were performed. Where are the others, why have they disappeared, and—above all—where is the song by the foremost figure in English music?"

"Who was?"

"I'll say no more. It's no great mystery. I ask myself about Stafford, why did he want this job? Virtually unpaid—only the flat and expenses, and though he makes up expense claims with the enthusiasm of an MP, they cover little more than his and Hazel's living expenses. So why did he want to come back to his ancestral home, not seen by him since 1939, and what was its particular appeal to him? I think that's all I want to say about that. See them out, Lesley."

Walking away from Oakdene, Sergeant Hargreaves was still trying to absorb the interview. "Doesn't strike me to be exactly a family lover."

"No. It seems to be the sort of setup where you love your family but don't like or trust most of its members," said Charlie. "They're not alone in that, though."

"Maybe not. But to practically accuse your own brother of stealing the family valuables . . ."

"Probably commonplace in Victorian times, that," said Charlie. "They had will-reading gatherings, and those often descended into fisticuffs. . . . I'm just worried we are going up some blind alleys."

"What do you mean?"

"We're looking into family rows, minor peculation, and low-level crime. What we should be looking into is—"

"Murder," said Hargreaves.

"Got it in one."

CHAPTER 11

Cherchez les Femmes

❋

Charlie left his car a hundred yards from the deepest part of Haroldswater pond. Not that any evidence of importance could still be in the area, such as prints or trinkets, but discipline demanded it. As he walked toward the rather unattractive feature of the landscape, a diver surfaced, looking like an overgrown seal, and presented something, which Hargreaves, looking as out of place as a rugby player at a synchronized-swimming event, took momentarily in his gloved hand and slipped into an envelope.

When Charlie approached him, Hargreaves's face was filled with what passed with him for excitement. "You've come at just the right time . . . sir."

"Good," said Charlie comfortably. "Not for nothing am I known as a lucky policeman."

"Oh, Gawd," said Hargreaves, almost spitting. "'Not for nothing am I known as.' I'll never get used to talking to you . . . sir. Your wife has a lot to answer for."

"Hurry, then. Spill the beans—to say it in your language."

Hargreaves began waving his fingers like a primary-school teacher. "Two things. First of all, the car. We don't know what it is—or was—yet, or the number, but it is not a Mini or an Austin Seven, or any of the little cars that us proles drove in former days."

"What do you mean by 'former days'? How old is the car?"

"The boys think prewar. We should be able to be more exact before very long. Apparently it's not only quite a big car—it's also, or was once, pretty posh. All the indications so far say 'class'—well produced, well fitted, real class. If I had that car before it went into the pond, I'd have been driving it to Brighton like a real gent. Even nowadays it's probably one of the all-the-rage cars of the prewar years. So good-bye to your theory that this was the deflowered kitchen maid, come back for her thirty pieces of silver."

"I seem to remember that was your idea, Hargreaves. And I liked it because it seemed to make other pieces fit. But remember, she's said to have been driving a car when she came back to Walbrook."

"Right you are, sir," said Hargreaves, who never wittingly lost possession of the ball. "What do you say to some sort of conspiracy?"

"Talk English, mate. What sort of a conspiracy?"

Hargreaves sat on a convenient rock. "Well, take it that this kitchen maid—name, sir?"

"Rose Patchett."

"Okay, Rose Patchett has been impregnated by the lord of the manor, name of Tim Quarles, the then-current representative of the family, owning and living in Walbrook. She has been paid off in the usual manner and on the usual scale: five shillings, a railway ticket to London, threats if she dares to bring back her own face or that of the baby to this part of West Yorkshire."

"Or the West Riding as it was then called."

"I didn't request a history lesson . . . sir."

"Anyway, that all figures," said Charlie. "Who might be the upper-crust figure she meets up with, who persuades her to get her claws into Timothy a second time?"

"Not the faintest idea, sir. It could be someone we don't know about. Someone Rose worked for who got all indignant at the way she had been treated. It could have been a sheer matter of conscience. What's the word you use?"

"Altruism? Disinterest?"

"Lovely. Sound really good. On the other hand she could have been in it for purely selfish reasons: getting her hands into the family fortune."

"Except that there was no family fortune, or hardly any. The seminars in the thirties improved prospects a little, but not hugely, and the moment war threatened, they were a dangerous thing to have been associated with. Notice that as soon as war came, the poets and musicians and that bunch got out and slipped off to the United States."

"Fair enough point," said Hargreaves magnanimously. "Someone we know of, then, or could have heard of. Someone who had associations with Walbrook, the house or the village."

Charlie was thoughtful when he trudged away to his car, and when he got back to Police Headquarters in

Leeds, he sat at his desk for a long time making notes. When Hargreaves came in, at the end of his shift, Charlie hailed him, across the large room.

"Hargreaves! Could I have a minute or two of your time?"

"I suppose so," he said, coming over. "There's only rugby on the telly tonight."

"I thought you'd be there with your can of lager and your eager sons."

"Rugby doesn't televise well, compared with soccer," his sergeant said, sitting down. "It looks like a game for thugs."

"Hmm. No comment. I've been thinking of all the women we've heard about or met on this case. It's possible that Rose Patchett had gone all upper-class with the proceeds of her pregnancy, but that seems unlikely in a girl of few talents. Who else do we know, bearing in mind that we don't know why the car went into the pond, and it could have been in any of the last seventy-odd years."

"What about the car, sir?"

"We don't know much yet, but remember cars last a long time, particularly posh cars; protected over the years by their posh owners. It could have been a vintage car when it went into the water."

"Fair enough, sir. Now—these women . . ."

"Well, there's Mrs. Wes Gannett—died or disappeared, we should be able to find out which."

"Got you."

"There's someone who I suppose we should call Mrs. Quarles."

"Sir Stafford's lady mum."

"Exactly. Said to have been gravely ill or alternately to be having it off with a local surgeon and any number of the participants in the seminars."

"Almost too fruity to be a suspect, sir."

"No one is ever too fruity. She could have been said to be gravely ill and then dead, all made up for the benefit of the children."

"Then there's this Mary-Elizabeth," said Hargreaves with a note of contempt in his voice. "Clumsy name."

"Names of the two queens before the present one, only they were queens by marriage, she's queen in her own right. But I see your point. It doesn't exactly slip off the tongue."

"Currying favor, sir?"

"I don't think the family was ever important enough to curry favor with royalty. They were too insignificant for Buck House to feel flattered."

"Are there any more?"

"There's an interesting fact I didn't know," said Charlie, leaning down toward his bottom drawer and pulling out a thick book. "Never despise *Who's Who*. It is not just the snob's delight, and it gives important crooks very nearly as much space as it gives important politicians, which is just as it should be."

"Get on with it, sir."

"And it is where I learned that Sir Stafford, in addition to being an expert on fifteenth-century Italian art and sculpture, a tireless pursuer of fakers and boosters of unjustified artistic reputations, had married—no year given—some coyness on Stafford's part, do you think?—one Hazel Quarles."

Hargreaves had to think about that.

"Meaning she was a Quarles when they married?"

"Yes. Either by birth or by an earlier marriage."

"They do seem to keep things in the family, the Quarleses and the Fienneses. Did they marry when they were both a lot younger?"

"I've phoned Mary-Elizabeth, and she says twenty years ago when they were both in their fifties."

"Mature that's called, I believe," said Hargreaves with a nasty chuckle.

"They could have married conscious that they had a common interest in the family and the house. Sir Stafford probably had some museum or gallery post and planned to retire soon when he was in his middle or late sixties. Nice pension, no doubt, but probably both had expensive tastes. The token-rental flat in Walbrook Manor must have been a big attraction."

"With full-time employment in the house and the convenience of being close to all the records of the history of the family."

"Which the other side of the family, represented by Mary-Elizabeth, was sorting into a fully publishable shape."

"Are you suggesting some kind of war between the two wings, just as, apparently, in the past?"

"I don't think I'm suggesting anything," said Charlie. "I don't understand well enough people like the Walbrook lot. Now I find that even Sir Stafford's *wife* is a family member. . . . Felicity thought that Lady Quarles was surprisingly open, and pretty much *au fait* with everything. But of course we have to treat her as suspicious."

"We have no case that involves Quarleses or Fienneses as yet," said Hargreaves.

"We have a swish car, dating back to the thirties in all probability, a time when Walbrook actually featured, in a very minor way, in national politics."

"I suppose so. No reason why Lady Quarles should be unable to discuss that, is there?" said Hargreaves. "You could talk to her if she was agreeable."

"I could," said Charlie unenthusiastically.

When Charlie arrived at Walbrook, he left his car in the lower car park, strolled up the grassy hill, not recognizing any of the dogs or their owners, and turned in at the Entrance Hall as a nice surprise for the ticket taker Felicity had introduced to him as Susan. When she saw him diving into an inside pocket, she protested.

"Surely you shouldn't pay—here on business."

"But I'm not. I'm here to see the First World War exhibition because it interests me. There's no reason to connect the house with the body in Haroldswater, is there?"

He looked at her with his policeman's eyes, and she swiftly backed away from the subject.

"No, of course not."

"Because if there is, we'd like to know."

"No, I'm sure there's nothing. I'd have heard."

But she had assumed he was there on police business, Charlie noted. He nodded and headed for the staircase.

Once on the first floor Charlie satisfied pretty quickly his desire to learn about the Great War. He lingered a little to take in the war's aftermath and stored in his mind the names of "arty people" (poets, composers, painters) who were affected by the terrible conditions and the horrific mortality rates of the four-year conflict. He registered that there were more paying customers than on the day that Felicity had come here, and he put it down to the inevitable surge of interest when a skeleton has been found nearby. When he heard the clatter of high heels, he went to the door: the exhibition had attracted primarily men, and the women who were there were mostly dressed in slacks and low-slung shoes. He saw the back of a woman of a certain age, straight-backed, and he thought he recognized Lady Quarles. She moved toward the little, roped-off staircase and put the rope aside gracefully and quickly. Then she replaced it and proceeded confidently upward. These were the actions of someone who knows what she is doing and has done it often. Not a shred of guilt at any unauthorized access.

Charlie waited five minutes or so, then walked softly to the stairway, put the rope aside in imitation of Lady Quarles's grace and confidence, and went up to the attic floor. He looked around at the improvised offices and storerooms. All the doors were shut to, but from behind one there were sounds—scuffling sounds of papers being roughly sorted through, files being shut. Charlie waited. Eventually he heard sounds of files being returned to shelves, and the door opened.

"Oh." Lady Quarles's slightly horsey face showed that she was taken aback.

"I took the liberty of coming up," said Charlie.

"Liberty as a visitor to the house, or as a policeman?"

"Initially as a visitor, then, when I happened to see you coming up here, as a policeman."

"There is no connection between the house and the bones everyone is talking about."

This jumping of hurdles from the house to the bones was done confidently, as if nobody was going to gainsay such an obvious proposition.

"That's what I said to the lady at the ticket office downstairs. But as I went round, I realized that it is not true. 'No known connection' would be more accurate. We have some remains, believed to be a woman's, apparently drowned while driving what, sixty or seventy years ago, was a very expensive car."

"Haroldswater is a mile and a half away."

"It is. But this is a rural area of modest houses. Even the National Trust has notably few houses in Yorkshire. Therefore it is something worth investigating: was there any connection between the dead woman in the expensive car and Walbrook? It seems possible because there are very few comparable houses within, say, a twenty-mile radius."

Hazel Quarles shrugged. "I don't want to quarrel with you. It's not a matter of any importance to me. Please look anywhere you want. With your permission I'll wait here till you've finished and then I can lock up."

Charlie nodded. But then he went off at a tangent.

"Did you know this house when you were younger, or was Sir Stafford's involvement in the Trust's formation the first time you saw it?"

Something close to a romantic glow could be seen in

Lady Quarles's eyes. "Oh, I knew it! It was a fairy-tale place to me in my childhood." Suddenly Charlie had a sense of her pulling herself together. "Mostly from photographs. I was very young."

Lady Quarles's attitude seemed to shift with a prevailing wind. "Of course. You must be. That terrible crime— though long ago, we heard, so hardly soluble today." When she got no response from Charlie she hurried on, "I'll just leave these papers. I came to restore them to their right files. Stafford sometimes takes things to read, or to finish reading. A bit naughty I'm afraid." This last was in response to Charlie's raised eyebrows. "He does rather think he is head of the house now and can do what he likes. Perhaps you could have a word with him."

"I think that is Wes Gannett's job."

"Oh, dear. They don't always—well, you know—see eye to eye. And Wes does have a colonial—no, I must keep quiet."

"I get your meaning. Could I see the papers—the ones you have in your hands?"

"Oh, I don't . . . Yes, of course. I was just bringing them back."

She abruptly handed the papers over and Charlie leafed through them. Many of them were of a financial nature and probably mirrored the family's difficulties in the twenties and thirties. Certainly the later papers suggested that the family's involvement in the peace movements of the time involved increased financial stability. Those papers, the ones concerning the new sort of expenses incurred, were often dealing with concerts, with fees paid to artists, of the need to make the concerts coincide with the seminars, which must have made many in the audience uneasily conscious that by mingling with the younger artists performing at the manor they were letting themselves be used as propaganda fodder.

"I'm sure these are quite harmless," Charlie said, handing them back to Lady Quarles. "But still I think they should be back in place. The last director got into trouble because of the archives and the records of family possessions, didn't she?"

"Something of the kind, I believe." It was stiffly said.

"It would be unfortunate if your husband was criticized for the same sort of thing, especially as his position, as a family member, makes him particularly vulnerable. People are very open to criticism if they can be seen as using their own special position for their own ends. It's largely unfair and springs from the MPs' expense scandals, but people are now very aware of possible conflicts of interest."

"But there's nothing of that sort about Stafford's looking into the manor's past. He's a sentimental old soul, and he loves his memories of the place from his childhood. He's just filling in the background of those memories. This taking of archives home—just one floor in fact!—springs from that, and when the item is finished with, and perhaps photocopied if it is really important, then it is meticulously put back either by Stafford or by me. Look—I'll put these back now."

She carried the papers that Charlie had offered to her into the little office. She took down two files and inserted the papers in the appropriate places, then marched out again, padlocking the door as if it were a garden shed. She turned to Charlie, then started down the wooden, uncarpeted staircase, but she stopped almost at once.

"You see, there was nothing very terrible, was there? Just a little piece of naughtiness from an old man. You will try and see that it goes no further, won't you?"

"If it doesn't have any reference to the case, it certainly won't go any further as far as the police are concerned," said Charlie.

"Thank you. You are very considerate. Please give my regards to your charming wife."

Charlie nodded briefly. Sir Stafford wasn't the only one who nourished delusions about being head of the family, he thought. His wife could be positively queenly. He hoped that his reply to her request had been sufficiently ambiguous to acquit him if he had to tell his superiors of any charge of lèse-majesté.

He raised his hand to Lady Quarles, then went down to the entrance lobby. "Could you supply me with paper and an envelope?" he asked Susan, in her place at the entrance. She smiled as she handed it over, and Charlie wondered whether she or another of the attendants could somehow have overheard the conversation in the attic and passed it on. If so, the subject matter would get around without him.

He wrote:

Dear Dr. Gannett,

I wonder if enough care is being taken of the house's archive. It is quite possible we shall want to

172

consult it on matters financial, artistic, or social. A little strengthening of the ramshackle structure in the attic might send out strong signals and would show that the archive should be taken seriously.

Yours,

C. Peace (Inspector)

CHAPTER 12

Medical History

∗

The next morning Charlie decided it was time to put in order the events of 1939—not how they affected the nation, but how they affected the Quarles and the Fiennes families. One source of information on Leeds and its checkered history was the private Leeds Library— "founded 1768, decades before the London Library," as it never failed to point out. Though Charlie suspected the only people who understood the catalog system were the librarians (and not always them), and though Felicity usually returned from working on the Victorian fiction there in a dusty state and foul mood, he had found its store of old newspapers and periodicals invaluable in the past. He rang them and asked the woman at the desk if there was such a thing as a history of Leeds General Infirmary.

"Not as such, no," she said.

"What do you mean?"

"There is a manuscript, several chapters long, written

by one of the surgeons there which we can sometimes get permission for one of our readers to consult."

"You don't have a copy yourselves?"

"No, they're very cagey. Or the author is. We asked if we could take a photocopy several years ago, but he said he wanted to keep control of who had access to the manuscript."

"Does he keep it himself?"

"Oh, no. It's in the infirmary's own library. A very flimsy typescript, and they've had to photocopy it them-selves to make sure it doesn't decay beyond retrieval. We'd like them to have taken a copy for us, but"—she sounded as if she was shrugging—"no permission from Dr. Winstanley."

"Dr. Winstanley. Surely that's not the one who worked there during the war and after?"

"No. It's his grandson. With one or two sections written by the grandson's father. There has been a real family tree of Winstanleys working there over the years."

"I see. So I could try the library there?"

"You could try. They're not wildly helpful, but, to be fair, there are special medical reasons—for example the right to confidentiality—which make difficulties for them."

Charlie put the phone down and pondered. He could not decide on the best approach to take. What was the reason for the fence around the history of an old, respectable institution such as the LGI? In the end he got on to the librarian at the hospital, explained that he was in charge of the investigation into the remains found in Haroldswater, and said he wanted to trace various connections with the Quarles family at Walbrook Manor. He was not interested in old scandals and would certainly not want to propagate them any further. She rang him back half an hour later. Mr. Winstanley had had a cancellation and a death before projected treatment and could see Charlie the same day from 2:00 till 2:45. Charlie thanked her gratefully—and noted what he had to do and where he had to go to see the Great Man—the present representative of the Winstanley family.

Mr. Colin of that name was sitting in his office with his feet up, speedily eating from one or other of three plastic-packed sandwich packets. He was a boyish fifty-odd, welcoming, well-spoken, and Charlie thought if he did ever contract cancer, he would choose to be treated by this man, or somebody like him.

"Sit you down," he said, waving. "Operating is a very hungry occupation, and starving yourself can lead to ghastly errors. That's what I find, anyway. You're investigating that Haroldswater skeleton, eh? Any news on the car?" When Charlie visibly hesitated, Winstanley put his big, capable hand up. "Don't tell me anything you shouldn't. I won't, so you shouldn't. I'd better tell you I promised when I started writing, just out of medical school and between jobs, that I'd say as little as possible about my grandfather, how he came to be chucked out—in the nicest possible way—and his various amorous entanglements. I've held to that ever since, and I'll try to today. But most inquirers are social historians, medical historians, and so on. Police investigating a possible murder are another matter entirely. Now—tell me about that car."

"Not much to tell yet because we haven't had time to haul in an expert on vintage cars. The essential fact is that we have the remains of a car, it is in style one from the thirties, it is very swish, and we have found no record of its being reported missing. Beyond that is pure guesswork. It could have disappeared roughly at the time the house—Walbrook Manor—changed hands, but stayed within the extended family of the original builder: the Quarleses and the Fienneses represent two wings of the family, usually at odds with each other."

Colin Winstanley sat, thoughtful, his fingers in a cat's cradle position now that they had finished the canteen's sandwiches.

"Any particular reason why it should be when the house changed hands?"

"Not really. The exchange was not amicable, it ended for a time any connections between the two wings. Tim Quarles had been an ambiguous figure with links to Hitler sympathizers, whereas the father of Rupert Fiennes, Montague by name, was an old-fashioned patriot with a strong interest in going to war, defeating the European fascists. Why do you ask?"

Again Winstanley considered over his cat's cradle.

"What happened to your 'swish' car when war broke out? I know a little about that because I wrote a chapter about the LGI in wartime. There were two possibilities when it became clear that the petrol supply was not going to be continued as far as private cars and their owners were concerned: *either* they were put to work for the public sector—they became emergency ambulances, attending on air raids, fires, and so on. The alternative was to put them into storage—mothball them. As with fine gates and railings which, rather than being melted down for the war effort, were put in the stables or the barns and tucked away nicely—not hidden, you understand—"

"Oh, no, of course not. Preserved for posterity."

Winstanley laughed. "Oh, yes, for the owner's posterity. You could call it a sort of patriotism: preserving the national heritage. But you can understand why Joe Average, the man in the street, didn't see it like that. Baldwin, the ex-PM, got quite a lot of flack by trying to save his wrought-iron gates from being melted down."

"Interesting. So what you're saying is?"

"Don't jump to conclusions about the car and the date of the incident. If it was mothballed in 1939 or 1940—the family pictures, the Lely and the Gainsborough, were put in a bank vault, the more bulky treasures would go into unused buildings, attics, even caves."

"And the great man concerned would pray that no question would be asked."

"Right. And even more to the point, extremely good care would be taken of the bulky treasure—the Bugatti or whatever—so that when in 1945 or '6 it was carefully removed from hiding, unpacked, and—hey, presto—"

"A car as good as new, ready to be driven again."

"Yes—if they could get the petrol. It was still rationed, but people in the know could still get hold of black market oil and petrol. It had to be done with care and sensitivity, but it was possible. And when it was—abracadabra! A new old car—flash, shiny, oozing speed and comfort, and hardly anything on the milometer!"

"I'm grateful for the explanation," said Charlie. "Do any names occur to you of people who might have done, or did, this sort of mothballing? Your father for example?"

"Grandfather. My father was an exemplary citizen, but he was still in his teens when war ended. No, you're quite right about my grandfather. He was the sort of man who drives a Rolls and says he regards it as a patriotic duty. That's what he did up to the declaration of war in '39, and again from '45. The great, the world-class surgeon supporting British industry by driving a gas-guzzling car. He was also, let's remember, a wonderful surgeon—that at least was true. So he had done a lot of favors in the past, brought about by fantastic surgery. If he wanted a car mothballed, there were always ex-patients ready and waiting."

"Is there anyone else in this part of the world with a connection to the Walbrook families who was likely to possess similar cars?"

"Well, you can rub out Timothy Quarles. Couldn't have afforded one. Left the area as soon as the house changed hands. Montague Fiennes had the money but was too careful of his image to flaunt an expensive car doing ten miles to the gallon. He was wanting to go into politics. Rollses were definitely out for such Tories in the late forties."

"Anyone else?"

Colin Winstanley thought again.

"Have you thought of Mrs. Isabel Quarles?"

"Is that the mother of Stafford and Graham?"

"Exactly."

"No, I hadn't thought of her. I thought they were one of the poor branches of the Quarles family tree. Then some seem to say she was mortally sick and died soon after the family's stay in the Dower House. She apparently had an affair with your grandfather—"

"Not apparently. That was for real."

"Yes. But it was hardly an affair likely to bring long-lasting riches."

"No. I'm not suggesting that. But first of all she didn't die. Not at the time of the change of ownership, nor yet immediately after the war. She and my grandfather were still meeting after the war. That was one of the reasons Granddad wasn't wanted when LGI was nationalized as part of the NHS."

"Why on earth was that? Not anyone's business but their own, surely?"

"True. What wasn't—or wasn't considered—their own business was the fact that she had left her family and set up as a high-class-brothel keeper in London. With an offshoot in Manchester by the by."

"Is that where the customer base was? I'm surprised by Manchester."

"What can you do when it's raining and all the

streets are up? Rumor has it she was planning one in Belfast."

"When was that?"

"About the time she left the scene. A year or two after the war she seemed to tire of the sex scene. First my Grandpa slipped out of the way. Wanted to put up a respectable facade for the Labour Party rulers. He was tired out as well: if ever there was a case of someone 'broken down by age and sex,' it was my grandpa, so they say. He managed to get most of the documentation of the enterprise out of the way though."

"But what about Isabel Quarles?"

"She just disappeared from the brothel scene. I'd guess she found herself a more permanent man than my grandpa and went off somewhere with him. They do that, whores. Just get tired of the life. It gets to be too much trouble to keep up the pace."

"And when was this?"

Colin Winstanley shrugged. "A year, a couple of years, after the war. My dad helped with the clearing-up of the premises. He told me about it much later. That was a big shock for Dad. He had to get a young doctor of vast experience to explain some of the things he found—sex toys and things."

"And what *was* the brothel—essentially?"

"Just a cover and side earner for Isabel's real business. There was some genteel blackmail, particularly of the politicians, but also of the big business chiefs if they were in the sort of business that had a healthy, family appeal."

"And what you're saying is that Isabel Quarles was the sort of woman—businesswoman—who might be driving a swish, gas-guzzling car well into the postwar years."

"I'm saying it's worth investigating."

"How would you describe her?"

"Mad, wild, daring, disobeying every code, moral or social."

"Nothing else?"

Colin Winstanley shifted in his seat. "Well, there must have been, mustn't there? If she was just the madcap I've described, no one would have paid up when she tried anything. She must have had a responsible, straightforward, trustworthy side, or nobody would have thought of paying up. They must have realized that if she said, 'So-and-so many thousand and that's an end to it,' she meant it and would enforce it. The victims probably came from a pretty restricted social background—people like Timothy Quarles, my granddad, top civil servants. They could do a bit of asking around in a dignified whisper, and when they found she was reliable, they paid up."

"And do you think she and Rose Patchett—"

"Who?"

"One of the maids at Walbrook who had Timothy's child and seems to have tried a bit of low-grade blackmail on him."

"Then in answer to your question, I doubt if any Yorkshire woman starting a brothel-and-blackmail in London would be wise to employ another Yorkshire woman. Down South, Northern accents are absolutely distrusted, and Yorkshire accents most of all. Very bad for business in all sorts of ways."

"But Isabel Quarles probably didn't have one," Charlie pointed out. "That class of person never does. They go away to school and have it ironed out of them. Take Rupert Fiennes and his cousin Mary-Elizabeth. I don't know if you know them, but they have not a trace of regional accent."

"I take your point. You could say I'm a victim of the same process. Yes, Isabel and Rose Patchett could have joined up. Or then Rose Patchett could have branched out with a few ham-fisted extra demands. 'Five shillings wasn't enough, I want more.' And it could have been her undoing."

Colin Winstanley glanced at the clock. "I can leave all that to you, can't I? You want to know about Isabel and I've told you all I know. I've got a bowel cancer to see to, so I'll sum up. Isabel marries a member of the Quarles family, a second cousin of Timothy, probably dull, certainly not well-off. She has children, does her family duty, then is ready to break free of the family. She has cancer, or possibly invents it, maybe even in cahoots with my granddad. The family come to live in the Dower House at Walbrook—it's where the poor relations were put; I learned that from my dad—and she went twice a week to see him in LGI. I'd bet a thousand quid she never paid him. When they went back home, life was intolerably humdrum for her. She had been spoiled by Rolls-Royces and top surgeons. She left hubby and the children and went to London. Maybe she took with her Rose Patchett, or more likely Rose was already there.

There was a war on, but war meant soldiers still more separated from female companionship than usual. There was a nice little income to be made. That, I take it, is the background. Any details about cars, pools, bodies, you will have to fill in yourself. I will go to my cancer, which is even more monotonous as a part of my profession than the male member probably was to Isabel and her profession."

"Thank you, sir," said Charlie. "I'll be as careful about what you've told me as I can be."

"It's not for me," said Winstanley. "It's for my poor dead father, who was sensitive on the subject. He thought people forgot his father's brilliance as a surgeon and concentrated on his various love lives. He never faced up to the fact that ''twas ever thus.' You can't make a cancer into a page-one story."

Walking back through the decrepit corridors and staircases of the Leeds General Infirmary, Charlie thought that this last comment was not quite fair: cancer can be a page-one story if the sufferer is well enough known. We live in an age of celebrities, alas, and few virtues and talents are needed to make a publicity-hungry man or woman into a national figure. And on a local level mere lust could make someone notorious. The elder Winstanley proved that.

Charlie scratched his head as he got in his car. Some other figure in the case resembled the eldest Winstanley in his pursuit of power or notoriety. Maurice something. Took over the song cycle after Ivor Gurney's death. Pursued the great and not-so-good for their contributions. No—he was not himself a celebrity but he was a hounder of celebrities. Maybe he was not an art historian, but he could well be a hoarder of dubious artifacts. Policemen in the past had ridiculed the existence of millionaire collectors who hoarded "hot" paintings and sculptures purely for the joy of having exclusive access to them. Could Maurice What's-it be one who serviced such men?

Worth finding a bit more about him.

CHAPTER 13

Art Nouveau

✳

Charlie didn't have many opportunities (wrong word, he said to himself) for contacting New Scotland Yard. A thick barrier of distrust and contempt existed between the policemen of the North and the South of England. To the South the North was a grim hellhole full of criminals with a gangland mentality, speaking in impenetrable dialect that would need subtitles if it ever got on television. To the North the South was a sewer crawling with drawling toffs whose own connections with metropolitan gangland made them near to impossible to work with.

Charlie, of course, had begun his police career in East London. He still had friends there, or people who had once been friends and could at a pinch be useful—especially if Charlie could turn the talk into an off-the-cuff briefing.

"Hello, Charlie," said Detective Inspector Janet Forster. "Congrats on your promotion."

"It took its time in coming," said Charlie equably. "But when it did come, it was very welcome."

"What can I do for you? Because I know—"

"I wouldn't ring you if I hadn't drawn a blank up here. There's a modicum of truth in that."

"'Modicum of truth.' I can tell you've got married to a writer."

"She'd be delighted to hear you say that. She gets quite shirty when people describe her as an academic. Right—here it is. I hear you do a lot of work for the stolen-art people these days. Is that right?"

"About ninety percent of my time's taken up with that."

"A man called Maurice Matlock. Ring any bells?"

"Plenty, but all very old and cracked. He must have died round about 1970."

"I thought he must be dead."

"But the surname lingers on."

"Matlock? I suppose I have heard of it."

"Martin Matlock. Arts correspondent of the *Daily Break*."

"Good God! Do they have one?"

"Oh, they have one all right. Wait—I'm just bringing him up on my computer . . . Oh, not very much. He seems to be a witness and an informer rather than a crim. There's a mass of headlines here—must be by him and designed to give us a good laugh. 'Covent Garden on the Game—Lulu's Back in Town.'"

"Who's Lulu?"

"The heroine of an opera by Alban Berg."

"Sounds as if it's a bit more bawdy than *The Marriage of Figaro*."

"Much more. 'Franz Comes Out of the Closet.' Concerns a ballet star, real name Sam Pitts, who wanted to stay in the closet for the sake of his old ma, but he reckoned without Matlock . . . 'Goings-On in the *Carry Ons*.' Sexual doings behind the scenes of the famous British low-budget smut."

"It's the puns that get me," said Charlie. "You have to be a moron to find them funny, but even more of a moron to think them up."

"You are attacking a fine body of craftsmen there, Charlie. . . . Let's see if there's anything more serious than bad puns."

"Hold on, Janet. Let's get this straight. Who is this cretin? What relation is he to the thirties Matlock?"

"According to him no relation at all. This is not generally believed, and there are various speculative answers: son, nephew, bastard."

"The last should be easy to prove. Why does everyone disbelieve him when he denies the honor?"

"Because he and the thirties man are so alike—not alike particularly in appearance, though there is a certain slimy resemblance, but in his interests: both are on the fringes of the arts world, getting what they can in gossip, and centuries-old speculations—'Was Mona Lisa a Lesbian?' sticks in the mind—and coverage of arts crimes, particularly picture thefts, if there is a sexual angle, or some suggestive angle concerning the well-heeled owner of the picture, or police incompetence."

"'Carry on, Constable,'" said Charlie. "I get the message. He springs to life immediately before us. What did you say his name was?"

"Martin Bernard Matlock—Marty to his readers. The father had Bernard as a middle name, so the connection didn't demand much in the way of guesswork. Still, he denies it."

"If the father was a dubious character, that's understandable."

"A bit silly, though, if it defies reason."

"Well, thanks for the help. I'll return the favor sometime."

"Maybe. Our dubious characters have been known to have taken refuge up North. They return white as sheets or orange from Permatan. They usually talk as if they've earned an OBE. Ciao. Charlie!"

It was Felicity who rang the offices of the *Daily Break*.

"Could I speak to Marty Matlock, please."

"He left the building half an hour ago. Won't be back till Tuesday."

"Any idea where he was going?"

"No, and I couldn't tell you if I had one. Though with that shitbag . . ."

"Was he going to one of the stations?"

"Yes. I heard him shout 'Euston' to the driver in his master-to-slave tones. Taxidrivers hate him. Can't help you any further."

Felicity rang her husband in Leeds, and half an hour later he came back with a suggestion about the so-called journalist's probable destination.

"First of all, the current newsworthy arts story centered on the Midlands is the return of the Hobden Lacy collection of three John Singer Sargent family pictures. Worth a lot, but not the fantastic sums you often hear of. Head of family denies he's paid a ransom, but is not generally believed. Head of family is married to a Russian multimillionaire's daughter. Used to be American dosh, now it's Russian. Family seat ten miles from Coventry. When he's in the area, Matlock usually stays at the Benison, Coventry. He's hated in all the hotels he's ever stayed at in the area, and Benison just covers it up better. See story with picture of the unlovely creep in today's *Daily Break*. Anything else you want?"

"Do they have a crèche in the Hotel Benison?"

"Yes. Good job, it's the Easter holidays. It'll be open. Take a gun with you—a nice little number with pearls on the handle."

"Don't indulge in fantasy. I'm not in any danger except of nausea. See you tomorrow."

Felicity's part in the Murder of the Unknown Woman case (the description of the *Times*) had been hatched up between Charlie and her the day before. She was not even to mention the police, but she was to emphasize her place on the Walbrook Trust, her feelings of worry, and so on. She and Charlie had talked things over ("But you're absolutely alone on this one," said Charlie) and decided it would be best to meet Matlock casually and not to pressure the encounter into interview shape or atmosphere. So here she was sitting flipping through vacuous Sunday color supplements in the hotel foyer with the door of the dining room kept well in sight. "Saves him trouble if he eats here," the receptionist said, scarcely bothering to disguise her scorn. At 8:40 he came down, and at 8:45 Felicity was seated at a table two rows away from her prey, awaiting an order of lamb chops (Lord Lucan's favorite meal, she seemed to remember).

Half an hour later, with a sorbet ordered to counter charges of dallying, she was looking at Matlock slurping down coffee after a meal served at double-quick by scowling waiters, keen to get rid of him. Felicity determined to disappoint them and went over to his table.

"If I bought you the most expensive brandy the hotel sells, would you let me talk business to you for a little while?" she asked, trying by her demeanor to make it clear that this was not an indecent offer.

Marty Matlock, inevitably, leered. "And what makes you think your purse, young lady, can buy me anything that my expense account can't match?"

To illustrate her point, one of the resentful waiters, with a particularly scornful glare at Felicity, came breezing over and slapped down a brandy balloon on the table. Marty Matlock sipped, assumed a satisfied expression, and signaled to the waiter to bring a second one at Felicity's expense.

"And what, my dear young lady, are we going to talk about?"

"Stately houses, and the trusts that look after them," said Felicity.

"Ha!" said Marty, apparently delighted. "You are on such a trust, elected to take care of the youth aspect. How to attract families, how to get more school parties, that kind of thing. But where is the crime suspect?"

"Possibly nowhere. If I'm there to represent youth nobody has told me I shouldn't dirty my hands with other matters as well. The house in question has been transferred from a private person into the hands of a trust. It is now open to the public. The trust has been recognized as a charity."

"And you think there is hanky-panky going on?"

"I wonder. We get in our meetings bare mentions of items from the collection that are away for cleaning or other treatment."

"Paintings?"

"Yes. Ramsays. Not all that valuable, but still . . ."

"You'd regret it if it came back as a forgery."

"Exactly. And the collection is nearly untouched by reliable research. There was work done under a previous director, but so badly as to be almost useless. We had a concert recently . . ."

"Oh, *yes?*"

"A collection of poems written specially for a project to cover the horrors of the First World War, organized in the late twenties, and still going by the time the Second World War broke out."

"Ah, yes. Now I see the relevance of the name Matlock."

"I'm not wishing to pry—"

"You wouldn't get anywhere if you were. I shall tell you nothing about my family background. But I am interested." And he did look it.

"You've heard of the project before, then?"

"Heard of it—and a bit more than that. We have come, I think, to the Manor of Walbrook in the County of West Yorkshire." He leered again. "Let's bare all, my dear. You know the place; I know it, though not well. And I know the chairman of your trust, Sir Stafford

Quarles. I have to say I've always thought of him as an impeccable *museum person*—to coin a phrase. I mean I think of words like *cautious, scholarly, impeccable*—all those dull words that I encourage the reader of the *Daily Break* to laugh at, or at least snigger at. To think of being scholarly about tables and chairs, writing desks and toilet dressers. But about someone like Sir Stafford I would try to be admiring and polite. He's been involved with fine furniture and pictures for nearly fifty years, and he's never been caught out in any jiggery-pokery yet. He's got one of the best records in the country."

"I see," said Felicity.

"You sound disappointed."

"It's not that. It's just that . . . well, if it's not him then—"

"Who is it? Well, for a start, the collection was in the hands of two of the Fienneses for six decades before the Trust came into being. They did let scholars and historians, amateur and professional, come and work in their library with very little supervision. Local people—cleaners for example—could be trained to look out for anything with a monetary value."

"Yes . . . I see," said Felicity.

"You are disappointed because you've got a theory and you're not willing to jettison it. But the most likely thing is that the missing things—the song, for an example—is somewhere in the collection in the attic, waiting to be found, filed under a quite ridiculous heading."

Felicity shot him a quick glance. "You know more than you've let on to. You're thinking that sometime in the future you'll be able to make a story of this."

"Sometime in the future?" His face took on its least attractive expression, that of leering self-approval. "Not so far in the future." He scrabbled in the briefcase that sat on the chair beside him. "Look—it's ready to be used when the time comes."

Keeping it as far from Felicity as he could, holding it delicately by its top corner, a rough print with the headline "The 'Patriots' with the Hotline to Hitler." It was illustrated by a picture of a man impeccably dressed and holding a champagne glass, standing by a boy/man whom Felicity thought she recognized as Benjamin Britten.

"I suppose that's Timothy Quarles, is it? I've never seen a picture."

"That's poor old Timmy, yes."

"And that's Benjamin Britten. I think you'd be hard put to justify the idea that Britten had a hotline to Hitler.

Marty Matlock sighed. "My dear, your ignorance of Fleet Street is appalling. I don't have to justify anything I say. I just have to present one or two facts or near facts—let's see, the fact that Britten was a pacifist throughout his life, and especially in World War Two, when he fought fires, after his return from America. He was also an attender of the peace-seminar weekends at Walbrook. Hey, presto! Britten was an admirer of Adolf Hitler and associated with all the least patriotic members of the art and music worlds. And then of course there's Peter Pears . . ."

"Don't tell me. Let me guess."

"Go ahead."

"He and Britten are like love and marriage, they went together like apples and pears. All the Britten operas have parts for children in them, in particular boys, and with a brief survey of the relationship with David Hemmings, the case is made. Oh, maybe there could be a sneer at Britten's surname—how inappropriate that he was Mr. Britten because he was no Chippendale . . ."

Marty Matlock regarded her benevolently. "You don't like me very much, do you, my dear?"

Felicity pulled herself together. "It's not for me to like or dislike."

"I wouldn't know that. I can only guess what you're doing this *for*, can't I? But I've always preferred being disliked to being liked. Prevents any emotional delusions on either side. Now you have had quite a large slice of my time for the price of a glass of brandy."

"A very good brandy."

"Admittedly, and horribly overpriced. So if you have no more questions . . ."

"Just one. What do you think the missing song in the *Trenches* song cycle consists of? Who wrote it, who wrote the words? Why is it apparently important eighty or ninety years after it was written?"

"Hmm. Difficult one. If you made the composer a highly desirable one, the best-known composer in the world, it still wouldn't amount to much in the twenties or thirties. There were no Beethovens or Schuberts then. Let's put it as high as seems likely: say the composer was Elgar, the song a powerful one, a plea for perpetual peace. It might just amount to Lady Quarles's dress bills for a year. It's easier to see the desirability of the manuscript in propaganda terms: it's not worth much, except emotionally. Elgar now, as then, would give *respectability* to Walbrook, respectability to the Quarles branch, and to all Timmy was hoping to do by spreading a pacifist message."

"Isn't Elgar much more popular now than he was after the First World War?"

"Oh, immeasurably. It's like Mahler: after the Second War nobody had heard of him, and he was good only for a brief sneer from the music critics. Now he's the greatest bar only Beethoven, and many would doubt whether *he* shouldn't be put down to second place. Same has happened more slowly with Elgar. Today every conductor worth his salt wants to record the symphonies, every cellist and violinist wants to record his concertos. What difference does that make, do you think?"

"By the sound of your voice, not much," said Felicity.

"Exactly. If he'd murdered his wife, or if some American suggests he did, the price of memorabilia would go up sky-high. Mozart always has a certain pathos because of being buried in a pauper's grave—which he actually wasn't. When it was suggested that he was murdered by a rival composer—whoosh! It's a mad world, my masters."

"So there was never much to be made by anything in the Walbrook collection?"

"I wouldn't say so. Luxury peanuts, but essentially still peanuts."

"So who do you think it was whose skeleton was found in the car?"

"Ah. That discovery. There's no reason to think there is any connection with Walbrook, let alone Walbrook in the thirties. The remains could be—just anyone! Someone's mistress. A spy. An inconvenient wife perhaps. An expensive leftover from the age of the flapper. Talk is that it's a woman. Reduces the suspect list by fifty percent. Big deal."

"But Walbrook is the only mansion—"

Marty Matlock held up his hand. "Spare me. Who said she was going there? Nobody. She could have been going from Mayfair to the Shetlands to escape the bombs. She could have been one of J. Arthur Rank's starlets on the way to Scotland to film a remake of *Greenmantle*. Anything is possible."

"So you don't even want to consider Walbrook a factor in that case?"

"Is there a case? . . . Oh, all right, young lady. Let's just forget about evidence, proofs rational arguments, and all those things that work against detective's flair in the sillier sort of crime book. Let's say the bones belong to someone who—I'm told—is the favorite candidate in Walbrook village for this upmarket corpse."

"And who is that who's told you?"

He played with her a little longer. "I am known for the excellence of my sources."

"Maybe a rather unusual trade-union representative whom I call Pink Trousers?"

Matlock roared with laughter. "Okay. You've earned my little driblet of information, which is no more than a piece of guesswork. I'd agree with the villagers and guess that the victim in the water was the mother of Sir Stafford Quarles. She was—"

"Oh, yes, I heard what she was."

"And if I was a policeman, and if I'd been given the hopeless job of investigating this crime, if there was one, I'd focus on that lady's life, and perhaps the life of her car, in two periods of her life."

"And they were?"

"The autumn of 1939 and the summer of 1947."

"I understand the first, but not the second. What was happening of importance in 1947?"

"The month war broke out in 1939 was the month that Walbrook changed hands from the Quarles branch of the family to the Fiennes member of the family. As you probably know, they didn't live in the house, but let it to the Defence Ministry for use as an asylum. It was handed back to the family in the autumn of 1947, but it had not been used as an asylum for some time, because there was not the same huge numbers of men with mental disturbance as there had been from trench warfare in the First War."

"What you're saying is that there were periods of interregnum when it would be easier than usual to get into the house and perhaps steal something that was known to be there?"

"Exactly. The intruder would probably have had an inside knowledge of the house. If she did, getting and taking whatever it was would have been comparatively easy."

"If she got there in the first place."

"If, indeed, she got there." He heaved himself up

from his chair, and relief showed on the faces of the few remaining waiters. "Thank you fcr your company, dear lady, but don't try to inflict it on me again. I shall sleep tonight with interesting thoughts of the Quarleses and the Fienneses. Not many people can say that. Good night."

CHAPTER 14

A Lady of Soho

✳

The next day, early in the morning, Charlie had an unex-
pected call from Colin Winstanley. Consultations and
operations had presumably not yet begun. The eminent
surgeon sounded almost apologetic.

"Inspector Peace. Sorry to ring you at this unearthly
hour."

"Don't worry about that, sir. I'm just collecting my
wits and my papers so that the new day can start."

"It's something I forgot, or maybe it should be 'something I didn't dredge up,' when we talked the other day."

"I'm interested in any of your memories."

"This is more my father's memories—or rather the
documentation of things I told you the other day. It
might give you a bit more idea of what was known at the
time, what managed to creep out to the general public."

"That could be valuable, sir."

"I hope so. I'm anxious to give all I can, in spite of
memories of what my father would have said. It's a long
time ago, and we might view my granddad slightly dif-

ferently now. . . . You won't remember the old *Daily
Telegram*—no, of course you wouldn't. They were a
broadsheet paper, respectable like the *Times* and the
Guardian, but they always made sure they got in all
the salacious details—in divorce cases, of known and
unknown people, rumors, royal scandals, political ones,
and it didn't matter what party the story concerned—
they'd print all the details."

"And your father aroused their attention, did he?"

"Yes. I think they'd been saving him up for a fair
while. Naturally you break your story with the best—the
most sensational I mean—aspects of the story. That's
what they did."

"When was this, sir? Was it some time in 1947?"

"I've been trying to think. Sometime about then I'd
guess. Was that when—"

"It's when the Fiennes branch of the family took back
Walbrook Manor from the government. We touched on
that earlier. It may also have been about the time the
accident—if it was one—occurred in Haroldswater."

"I see. I understand your interest. Well, I would guess
a week or two after the handover—that's a guess—the
Telegram started printing stories about gossip in the
society world of a high-class brothel—they didn't call it
that though—in Soho, run by a woman of good repute
in a setting—in spite of its being in Soho, *just*—of the
utmost style and class, with educated and well-brought-
up girls and women among the offerings, including a
child reputed to be the madam's own daughter."

"Really? I'm not sure I'd heard that she had a daughter."

"That figures. Isabel went in for fakes, false fronts. Anyway, after a few more titbits the newspapers shifted their focus. They were now linking the story with a well-known doctor, a surgeon, and of course he had to be a 'society' doctor, or surgeon as he in fact was. They finally got around to the point: he was, with Madam Crécy as she called herself, the joint proprietor of the establishment. He paid half the rent and took half the profits."

"Surely a pretty suicidal thing for a doctor to do, wouldn't it be?"

"I'd have thought so. Especially then, with the National Health Service coming into being. But I think I'll stop my story there."

"Oh? The shadow of your father looming?"

"No, not that. But I've never seen the newspaper coverage. What I've told you was pure gossip within the family. It could be spot-on, the newspaper stories could have been accurate, but I think you ought to go to the *Telegram* archives, wherever they may be, and see exactly what they said, and go on from there. I might mention, because the *Telegram* may not, that my grandfather lived to a fairly highly respected old age, with tributes from his fellow medics, full of praise for his professional brilliancy, and for his 'lust for life.' Yes, I was amused that phrase was used. Now I'll leave it with you."

And Charlie thought that that was a sensible line for him to take, and one he was grateful for: he wanted to get at least the bare bones of the story without family piety intervening. In seconds he got on to Pink Trousers.

"Mr. Wheeler? Will Wheeler? This is Inspector

Peace. . . . There is something not very vital I thought you might remember your father talking about. . . . Yes. I realize you heard a lot of stories. Can we see if this is one of them? I want to know exactly—or as exactly as you can make it—when the Manor of Walbrook was handed back to its owner after the war. . . . to Montague Fiennes."

He waited, tactfully saying sweet nothings when Pink Trousers said, "I'm working on it." Eventually he came up with all he could remember hearing of the transfer.

"I was born just after the war—well, nine months or so after, not to be too coy about it. . . . Yes, a VE baby, born in February '46. Now the manor was still being used—underused my father used to say—as an asylum as they persisted in calling it. The handover took place in the next year, toward the end of it. I remember my father said the winter of 1948 happened just after the Fienneses took over again, and the old man—Montague Fiennes—used to complain to high heaven about the incidental expenses like snow clearance, means of heating the place, and so on. It was really a bad time for everyone, and the large, wide-open spaces of parts of the manor didn't help."

"You said winter of '48," said Charlie. "Does that mean the winter that started in late '47?"

"Yes, it does. If you want to pinpoint the date the manor was handed over, I'd say sometime in November or early December of 1947. Dad always talked about how the snow came to bring another misery to the third austerity Christmas of the postwar era."

"You say it with relish," said Charlie. "Like a politician welcoming bad news."

"Not welcoming at all. All the earliest Christmases I have memories of were ghastly. It was only when I started getting my own friends, if you take my meaning, that I began to see the point of it."

"So if anyone came to the manor at that time, it was probably to see Montague Fiennes, or conceivably the last of the inmates, though I believe most had left already, or, still more likely, to retrieve something left there in 1939."

"Spot-on, I'd say—not having your training of course."

"Any ideas what they might have been after?"

Pink Trousers thought. "There are one or two of the pictures worth a tidy sum now. What they'd have been worth in 1947 I've no idea, but I'd guess not very much. The old landed gentry couldn't have been more out of fashion, according to my dad, and they only started making a comeback later, in the fifties—the Macmillan era."

Charlie rang off, then sat pondering. Then he rang one of his favorite places, and half an hour later he was seated in a secluded niche in the privately owned Leeds Library, poring over fragile copies of the *Daily Telegram* for the second half of 1947.

He found what he wanted pretty soon—a tribute to the union man's guesswork. Each issue of the daily was thin, now brown in color, but it did cover a remarkable amount of politics, sport, regional news, international developments, and sex. The last was inserted under all sorts of headings, and it found a place in the humorous column "Funny Old World." There, Charlie came upon a photograph of a woman he felt resembled someone he had recently seen. The face was all that was shown, but it seemed to be cut from a large group, because either side of her, there were traces of curled hair, perhaps of female children, their heads reaching her shoulders. One resemblance that Charlie saw in a few seconds was to the lady he thought of as the queen mother—then the queen of the wartime king, George VI. He quickly decided the resemblance was mostly a matter of hairstyle, makeup, little hat to the front of her forehead: a fashionable look, he decided, in 1947.

The image the lady presented was of a fashionable, wealthy, and distinctly hard personality. If children had been in the original of the same photograph, they must surely have been there to soften the image. The paragraph under the picture said that "social life" was picking up after the trauma and disorder of war, and salons were starting to form themselves not around the current Labour government, of course—they would scorn the institution—but around the old aristocracy and gentry, flexing their elegant muscles and hoping for a new general election. The so-called Lady Crécy was one of the foremost of these pioneers. That was all. But already Charlie felt he smelled a rat. If the children had been there as a softening feature, why had the *Telegram* cut them out?

The story was almost immediately revealed as a negative one. Three days later, a headline read "Woman of Mystery" and the article pointed out that Lady Crécy was not an English title, that titles in France had no legal existence, and the French aristocracy were notably snooty and almost invariably married one of their own.

Two days later the headline read "Ho-Ho Who's Your Lady Friend?" The quote was from a music-hall ditty, hinted at sexual impropriety, and could as easily have come from the *Daily Mirror* as from one of the broadsheets. In the shady part of a picture of a door the shape of a man was huddled—with just part of his face lit up by an outside light. Charlie did not find the man recognizable, but his looks and his clothes did seem to proclaim the description of *gentleman*. Who was it? he wondered. A Tory MP? A Labour cabinet minister? Or it could be a well-known surgeon? Whoever it was, it was clear that the *Telegram* was playing games with him. And with her of course—the madam of the surely high-class brothel.

The next reference that Charlie found proclaimed "The Wicked Lady"—the title of a scandalous Margaret Lockwood film. The same picture was used as in the first reference to her, though one could see more of the child on the lady's left, who was revealed as about nine or ten years old, pretty in an upper-class sort of way, and pensive—almost, it seemed, melancholic. What was a child of that age, Charlie wondered, doing in a brothel, or at least in the company of a brothel's madam? And why did the story come to an end in the last week of November 1947? For the last reference to the lady and her career choice was the bewildered: "Where Is the Wicked Lady?" The newsprint read, "What has happened to the so-called Lady Crécy? She has disappeared from her place of work, her 'staff' seem to have no knowledge of where she is. Where is she, and what sort of business did she run? We will report to you anything we hear about her, and the glittering circle of politicians and others who cluster around her." But as far as Charlie could tell, they never did.

As he walked back to Police Headquarters at Millgarth, Charlie thought over his conduct of the case, with some dissatisfaction. He remembered advice he had given Felicity as gradually she became involved in the affairs of Walbrook Manor, and he thought that he had not followed his own rules. He had assumed that Sir Stafford was an amiable old buffer whose innocence of real crime having to do with the bones in the car or anything else could be assumed. The same *mutatis mutandis* (he rolled the delectable phrase around on his tongue) had been applied to Lady Quarles. He had been influenced, of course, by the fact that, even as the wreckage of the car and the stock of bones accumulated, there was no "case," and that they were only at the stage of deciding whether one could be put together. Charlie decided it was well past the time when he should have talked to Sir Stafford.

When he had snatched a brief and horrible lunch in the police canteen, Charlie got in his car and drove out to Walbrook Manor. He had no advance knowledge of Sir Stafford's whereabouts, but he was delighted to be told he was in his flat and meekly accepted directions there, which he did not need. When he knocked on the door, the welcome in Sir Stafford's tone was distinctly underwhelming.

"Ah, Mr., er . . . Inspector Peace. What can I do for you?"

Not very much it seemed from the stance that he took up in the opening between the door and the wall. Sir Stafford could not himself be physically impressive, but he had had a lot of experience in putting people in their places, and it showed.

"I wonder if I could come in and have a brief c—"

"I am extremely busy." End of conversation he apparently hoped.

"And so, Sir Stafford, am I. I feel I should have talked to you before now. Let's go inside and get it over with as quickly as possible. This is not the sort of interview I'd want to get a warrant for, but if—"

"Oh, come in. Come in. Sit down. I'm sorry to be short with you, but I really do have *immense* amounts of work, of all imaginable kinds. But still, let's get down to it."

Charlie sat down. He had had time by then to look around the flat and note that it did not justify Lady Quarles's claim to poor housekeeping. With the exception of the occasional file on the table in front of Sir Stafford's armchair, which was littered with reference and art books, the room was conspicuously neat, and with no attempt at grandeur. Contrary to some earlier suggestions, the couple apparently did not wish to assume the pretense of the lord and lady of the manor. Administrator of the most usual kind, the room seemed to announce.

"Where exactly did you live, Sir Stafford, when you stayed here with your father and mother in 1939?" Charlie began.

"The Dower House." Still snappily.

"And you were about three and stayed here some while?"

"About four months I've been told."

"So it could be said Mr. Timothy Quarles was very good to you."

"It could indeed," said Sir Stafford, thawing just a little. "And I think I can say we were grateful. I know my father always spoke well of Timothy Quarles, who was a distant cousin and thought his kindness eased the business of my mother's illness."

"I've never heard what she was suffering from."

"It was cancer. There were a lot of other words for it then, but that's what it was, and the words didn't hide it at all."

"It's been represented to me that we should be concentrating our attention on two dates in the history of the house."

"The house? If you are investigating the car accident at Haroldswater, then I don't see what the house has to do with it."

"Bear with me. The two dates are September 1939—"

"The change of ownership," said Stafford, ignoring the little matter of the war.

"And the autumn—I think early November—in 1947."

"I don't know any significance to the house of that date."

"The time when it was handed back to the family after being used as an asylum during the war."

"Oh, yes. It's difficult to forgive the appalling Montague Fiennes for that act of vulgarity. Quite unnecessary."

"I think many much grander stately homes were commandeered by the politicians for use during the war."

"Commandeered. Not handed to them on a plate. But you must think me very petty. It comes from my love of the houses, and of the people in them."

"When did your mother die, Sir Stafford?"

"*When?* Oh, I was very young then. I can't put a date to it, but it must have been early in the war. It left me and my brother more or less alone with my father, who was not the best companion for a young child. He half realized this and sent my sister away to grow up in Canada, with relatives."

"Sister? Tell me about your sister."

"A year older than me. We've never got in touch. I have no memory of her, nor she of me, probably. There seemed no point in making contact."

This from a man who proclaimed his love of the houses and the inhabitants of gentrified England.

"Sir Stafford, you say your mother died of her cancer early on in the war."

"That's right. I remember my father calling me into his study and telling me. I remembered so little about her by then that I hardly shed a tear."

"You feel differently now? That it was a great loss?"

"Of course. Surely everyone who loses their mother in early childhood must feel loss. Sending me and my brother away to boarding schools made things worse, not better."

Charlie shifted in his chair. He found he could not avoid clumsiness.

"Would it surprise you, Sir Stafford, to hear that people who have told me about your mother have assured me that she was still alive after the war—at least until 1947?"

Sir Stafford's face assumed the fishlike look faces do assume when their surprise is genuine.

"Alive? After the war? Of course that's nonsense. I was told by my father. He couldn't have been mistaken. Would never have told me a lie."

"Perhaps he felt that the lie was the kinder thing."

"The kinder thing? But how could that be? I don't know . . . I don't understand. . . . What could be worse than dying of cancer? You seem to . . . Are you imply- ing—?"

"I must be blunt. What my informant was imply- ing—stating directly, in fact—was that your mother left the family circle about the time you and your father went home from Walbrook. I imagine the word was put out that the cancer was inoperable. In fact she had left her husband, left you, your brother, and your sister, for another man—perhaps more than one man. It was wartime—a time when normal sexual behavior is for- gotten and the main object for many people is having a good time."

Charlie had been looking away from the pathetic figure in the chair opposite him. Now he looked back and was horrified to see the old man struggling to rise, and reaching shakily for a stick that apparently he kept beside his chair to be used at need. Sir Stafford seemed to think that need had come. His breath was noisy with outrage, and his glance was fiery and unforgiving.

"You are trying to tell me that all I've ever been told

about my mother was untrue. It is outrageous. You seem to be telling me that my mother did not merely have an affair, but that she was a woman of easy virtue." Only with difficulty did Charlie repress a smile at the wonderfully dated phrase. Sir Stafford took a step forward to try to seize the stick. "How dare you, sir? How dare you?"

With relief, Charlie heard a key in the door of the flat. Sir Stafford looked in that direction, and the relief that Charlie felt was mirrored in Sir Stafford's face at the sight of his wife.

"Whatever is happening? Inspector Peace, what do you think you're at? My husband is an old man—how can you think of upsetting a man of his age and distinction. There, Stafford, there. Come and lie down."

The two figures, brave yet pathetic, disappeared through a door into a bedroom. Charlie sat down again. He felt he had not distinguished himself. Only the fact that he was dealing with a possible crime, perhaps murder, could excuse the brutality of his approach. Or had he just been fooled? Had Sir Stafford known about his mother all along, or perhaps from his adolescent years or early manhood?

If so, he had put up a good semblance of shock. The door to the bedroom opened. Lady Quarles sailed majestically in, her face expressing, or feigning, outrage at seeing Charlie still there, invading their domestic territory.

"I think you should go, Inspector. I think you should already have gone."

"I understand your feeling. I couldn't quite believe

that your husband could live a long life without somebody enlightening him about the nature of his mother's reputation. You are aware of it, I assume?"

"I'm aware of many things that are better not discussed, Inspector. Stafford's mother was a marginal figure on the fringes of the country gentry. For a few years after she left the family home, she lived in London—a rackety life that anyone, not just family, would rather forget about. The family said she was dead, and people shrugged and forgot about her."

"But I am investigating a death, perhaps a murder. I can't just accept convenient lies."

"Do you have to be so cruel, Inspector?"

"I'm afraid I do. I'd guess that when you married Sir Stafford, you were still in the accepting-convenient-lies stage."

"I was. I'd only known him two or three months. As I got to know him better—and *love* him too—it became clear that his loss of his mother was part of a treasured memory, with Walbrook Manor at the center. His time here as a little boy, combined with glimpses of the house later in childhood and adolescence, was the great experience of his life, the ruling passion. That's when I say again, you are cruel, quite unnecessarily cruel."

"How could I possibly put in the witness-box someone who thought his mother died of cancer in 1939 when in fact she lived on in London under a false name, or several, ran an upper-class brothel, and may well have died in a car accident some years after leaving home—an event that could well be something more than an accident."

"Do you *really* think your investigation is going to lead to a criminal case? After all these years?"

Charlie shrugged. "Perhaps not, but I have to act as if it will. Sir Stafford's father must have connived at the deception about his wife's disappearance, so he was certainly involved in a way your husband is not. You have not told me how you came to see through all your husband's talk about his mother."

"I haven't told you, and I don't intend to tell you. It would be a gross piece of treachery to do so. It involved the grandson of the man—a fine surgeon—who was let's say associated with her. I intend to let my husband cling to his illusions, if that is what they are, and I shall proceed as normal in the hope that nothing comes of the car in Haroldswater. I would say I was pretty safe that nothing ever will."

Charlie turned and looked at the determined old face, strong, good-looking. "There's something else, isn't there? Something other than your desire to preserve your husband's illusions."

"Nothing that I'm sure you haven't guessed. My husband grew up clinging to the illusions about Walbrook, and they were illusions in which he played a part. He was second cousin once removed of Tim Quarles. He formulated a fantasy which he soon came to regard as a fact that he was the rightful heir to Walbrook. He clung to this even though solicitors and legal men of all shapes and sizes tried to convince him there was nothing in it. It wasn't like a monarchy, with 'next in line to the throne.' So when he accepted the job as chairman of the Trust, he insisted the flat—*this flat*—

be carved out for us, a perfectly sensible suggestion, but it would have been even more sense for it to be the home for the director. Since we moved in, Stafford has identified himself more and more as the representative of the old family rather than as the museums expert with a long line of prestigious appointments to his name. I aim to continue to support him in this, Inspector Peace."

"That is what I would have expected, Lady Quarles."

"And you and your grubby little investigation can go hang. That is all the help from me you will get."

"I'm very grateful for it. You know, I think you should try to remember that if my investigation is grubby, the grubbiness springs not from the police going about our normal business, but from members of your husband's family. And of course, of yours, Lady Quarles."

She looked daggers at him for a moment, then pretended to have heard a noise from the bedroom. At the door she turned and looked significantly at the exit door. Then she went to her husband and Charlie had nothing to do but leave.

On his way down to the stables car park Charlie began thinking. First he wondered what place Lady Quarles actually had in the checkerboard of the Quarles and Fiennes family. Sixtieth cousin forty times removed? Still, it did seem fitting that Sir Stafford should choose to take to wife (first wife? he wondered) one of his own family. To hell with inbreeding fears—like should cling to like.

Then he began to think that, judging Lady Quarles

simply from her appearance, the tones of her voice, her relationships, he would have thought she should be much more interested in money than in family prestige. She looked healthier than Sir Stafford, almost certain to survive him. Old age was made tolerable by money, as often as not, and a good family tree buttered few parsnips.

Could it be that Lady Quarles was influenced in all her actions and attitudes by the possibility of discovering at long last some piece of treasure that could be sold in secret and render her last years comfortable to the point of luxury? He couldn't prove anything, but to him that motivation made a lot more sense than the family obsession with birth. Whoever really prospered on the branches of a family tree without the support of property, shareholdings, or personal art collections?

Looking back at what he had learned of the progress of the Walbrook Trust since its formation, he could see ample grounds for his diagnosis of money lust. There had been the appointment of the first director, who had had (had been encouraged to have?) an obsession about cataloging the collection. When this had progressed some way, she had been sacked and the cataloging only continued by the haphazard exertions of Mary-Elizabeth Fiennes, who had neither qualifications nor any depth of historical knowledge. The classification of the collection had never got off the ground. Was there the hope that the collection would throw up something of real value, with the corollary that it could be removed from Walbrook (for example as being of dubious authenticity) and a lucrative market found for it?

And as Charlie resumed his walk, other clues to what

had happened came into his head: the photograph in the *Daily Telegram*; the date of the transfer of Walbrook back to Montague Fiennes; the disappearance of the brief Elgar song . . .

By the time he was belting himself into the driver's seat, he was feeling a lot more pleased with himself, and pleased with his conduct of the impossible case.

CHAPTER 15

Emergency

✳

Three days, and a lot of routine inquiries later, the most enthusiastic components of the Trust Board assembled in the little parking area by the stables and waited for the door to be unlocked. Wes Gannett was also there, but was apparently not sufficiently senior to open the door. They had been summoned by a round-robin nowadays called a memo from the chairman of the board, who said that matters of the utmost importance had arisen since the last regular meeting and it was essential that decisions be taken as a consequence of these emergencies. Sir Stafford had sent out the summons, but he had not yet made himself visible. One of the board members had parked her car in the regular house car park and had seen there a car with a youngish black man inside studying papers. It was Maya Tyndale who had seen Charlie, and she said nothing about it to anyone, beyond a glance with a wink in Felicity's direction.

At one minute past the appointed hour of ten o'clock the chairman of the Trust appeared from the main

218

door of Walbrook Manor and began the descent to the stables. His walk was like his usual walk—light, commanding, spry for his age—but his descent had a Day of Judgment air that by the time he arrived at the stables ensured that all the ambient chatter had ceased.

The meeting began with an almost magisterial banging on the table. Sir Stafford's gavel hand had seemingly gained in power and determination.

"I declare this special meeting of the Walbrook Trust Board in session. I have asked the museum director to take the minutes, and you have agreed, have you not, Wes?"

"Provided there is nothing controversial about matters that come within my sphere of interest and for which it would be better to have a more neutral person take them." Wes sat himself down coolly beside the chairman.

"Precisely. I think I can assure you that will not happen. This is purely a board matter, not a museum one." Wes Gannett pursed his lips, as if to reserve judgment on that: complicated spheres of influence did not usually divide themselves so neatly. "The matter I feel strongly about, and about which I would like a stern and clear directive from the board, is the matter of the skeletal remains found in the car in Haroldswater. I don't think any of you could be ignorant of the fact that Walbrook Manor has been dragged into this police case, where the investigation is in the hands of Inspector Peace. I used the expression *dragged into* because there is not the slightest reason why we should be involved. I cannot ignore the fact that one of our board members is married to the detective inspector."

By now Felicity had foreseen what was coming, had exchanged glances with Maya Tyndale, and knew what she was going to say.

"Would you prefer me to leave the room, Mr. Chairman? Perhaps everyone would then be freer to say whatever they want to say."

"I think that might be wise, Mrs. Peace—"

"Wait a minute," came the voice of Ben Hooley. "Isn't that too much like a guilty verdict being pronounced before a trial has been conducted? Felicity may have information that can help us. She needs to be present to tell us what is true, what is not true, and what her explanation is of how Walbrook Manor has become involved in this police investigation."

The chairman looked daggers at Ben Hooley. "I bring this matter to the board because I could not legitimately deal with it myself. The investigation of the Haroldswater remains has led to a preposterous suggestion: that the skeleton in the car is that of my mother, that she did not die in 1939, which has been accepted by everybody for almost the length of my lifetime, but lived on until at least 1947. What purpose she could have had in driving to Walbrook at that date, when the house had been taken over by the Fiennes family"—he gestured toward Rupert, whose face was twisted into a grimace—"I don't know, but I imagine some suitably impossible reason has been thought up."

"It seems to me that rather than Felicity, the person who has an interest in this matter," said Ben Hooley, "is in fact yourself, Chairman. This must be an extremely painful matter to you, but in the end you cannot lead a meeting which is bound to cover such personal ground for you."

"You take it very calmly, this calumny of my dear mother," said Sir Stafford. Felicity was unable to decide how seriously to regard his anger and sorrow. "My mother came to Walbrook in 1939 as a last resort, and with a terrible and painful illness, which medical science at that time knew very little about, and hardly anything about treatments or cures. So do you wonder at my grief when the suggestion is made, which the police apparently believe and which you all no doubt will hear, that my mother somehow lived on, became a woman of dubious morals on the streets of London, sold herself to politicians and men of influence? I suppose the next allegation will be that she was in the pay of Adolf Hitler."

He looked around, outrage written clearly on his face. Felicity did not say that the possibility was not altogether fantastic.

The meeting began to descend into a cacophony of shouting and banging on the table, and it was not immediately noticed that another figure had come through the door. Charlie advanced on the table, took the one empty chair, and sat down, looking around him.

The cacophony immediately resumed.

"This is outrageous behavior," Sir Stafford spluttered. "Even a policeman has no right to invade a private meeting—"

"I have not only invaded the meeting, I shall forthwith end it."

"You have no right—" began the chairman.

"I have every right," said Charlie, taking from his file a

sheet of photocopied paper. "It is clear from the Articles of Association for the Trust that special meetings of the board may be called provided that all members of the trust receive advance notice of the meeting of at least seven days. This is to avoid the meeting being surprised into voting on a matter it has not been prepared for. Felicity received three days' notice"—Charlie looked up; several heads were nodding that they had received the same—"so this meeting has been, from the beginning, illegal, a contravention of the Articles. We can forget about rules and regulations. Let me suggest that we start the informal meeting with the subject the chairman himself no doubt feels most strongly about: his mother."

"There is no call whatsoever to discuss her," said Sir Stafford.

"I think there is. The first fact is that your mother finished her treatment at Leeds General Infirmary in July 1939. The family, father, mother, sons—you, Sir Stafford, and Graham, your brother—and daughter, returned home to North Yorkshire, then called the North Riding. A matter of two or three weeks later your mother was back in Leeds. I have consulted the grandson of the surgeon who treated Mrs. Quarles. She had a benign tumor that was known to be such from the beginning of treatment. She was, on her return to Leeds, staying at the surgeon's expense at the Queen's Hotel. With the countries of Europe on the brink of war, she subsequently went down to London—rather brave of her, with air raids a certainty sooner or later—and set up a recreation center for soldiers and politicians: in short, a high-class brothel."

There was an immediate uproar in the room, through which Charlie could hear Sir Stafford's outrage: "Not true. A damnable lie."

"Not a lie. Everything is confirmed by the police action centering on your mother that Scotland Yard began in November 1947, two and a half years after the end of the war. Her establishment by then was in a rented house overlooking Regent's Park. The front to the world was respectable, and the woman known as Lady Crécy had two children to give a family feel to what went on there. The so-called Lady Crécy provided high-quality meals, games, conversation to the MPs, civil servants, and servicemen. The police knew the basic facts of her services and turned the other way. MI5 had investigated and reported back that they could see no sign of treasonable behavior in her activities, but they cautioned that Lady Crécy would do anything for money."

"Lies! Lies!" muttered the chairman.

"Now we come to the question of Lady Crécy's death. A few relevant facts. When the police started investigating her disappearance—off their own bat, not called in by the staff at the establishment—the detective inspector was told that she had traveled to the North, and that it was 'a family matter.' Perhaps for that reason she took with her the two unidentified young girls who had lived with her for several years. At some point in the journey to Walbrook the children must have been left somewhere. There has been no trace so far in the investigations of the remains of any other than that of a middle-aged female. So we have two children—two girls that we hope have grown up—unaccounted for. We have noted in the course of our investigation the existence of several women with connections to Walbrook whom we would like to contact but cannot. There is Mr. Rupert Fiennes's wife, who long ago divorced her husband—"

"Now married to one of the top brasses in the army, shouldering the burden of our men in Afghanistan. I sometimes see him on the television news and I think 'poor bugger'—not because he's married to my ex-wife but because he's leading the army in an impossible situation."

"No contacts between you?"

"None since I became a civilian."

"Right. And then there was Mr. Gannett's wife, apparently dead."

"Not apparently," came Wes's voice from a reddened face. "She died eighteen months ago. The worst thing that could have happened to me."

"There can be worse things than death. Cases of premature senility bring hideous unhappiness both to the person concerned, and to his or her immediate family. I suggest that the moment the diagnosis was made, your wife pressed you to say she was dying, said she wished to suffer the horror of her condition on her own, so your memories would all be of happiness. That is what has happened, isn't it?"

After a pause Wes Gannett nodded miserably.

Charlie took up his story. "She is now living in the Westcliffe Nursing Home just outside Torquay—moderately healthy in body, nearly disappeared as to mind. I have spoken at length to the lady who owns and runs the place—a notably good, much-praised institution."

Wes Gannett groaned, put his head on the table, his shoulders heaving. Then he pushed back his chair and ran for the door.

"Leave him," said Charlie. "He's facing up to the horror of his wife's situation—maybe *really* facing up for the first time. Now one last woman, one who had been almost left out of our consideration. I knew little until recently of her existence." He looked around the assembled board. "Her name is Mary." His eyes stopped at Rupert and his cousin. "And we have in this inquiry one whose name is Mary, which she changed long ago into Mary-Elizabeth—with hyphen. Is that not so, Mary? You were, until you were taken to London by your mother, the so-called Lady Crécy, a pure and simple Mary, but you added the name of the queen—of the king's wife, which was also the name of the heir to the throne."

Mary's eyes were still sharp but her voice had a pleading note to it now. "Could we talk about this in private?"

"Of course. Would you like anyone with you?"

"My cousin."

"Not your brother?"

"No. No disrespect, but I know and love my cousin. I hardly know my brother."

She got up hurriedly and pushed open the doors to the outside world—the real world. Charlie wondered how many of the realities of the world Mary-Elizabeth was aware of. Charlie made his excuses to the stunned board members, and he and Rupert Fiennes followed behind.

"Our flat?" Rupert queried. "She hates it, but she'll feel safer there."

"Good idea. Should we tell her?"

"Oh, she'll guess that I've suggested it. We know each other's minds."

And she did indeed lead the way to a three-story Victorian house, heavy rather than dignified, but holding a newly decorated flat with the all-mod-cons of the traditional advertisements. Charlie looked and approved.

"Would you like a cup of tea?" asked Mary-Elizabeth. "Or coffee?"

They settled for tea and she bustled out to the kitchen. Charlie wondered whether this was the opportunity to discuss what was coming, but Rupert said, "I think you should allow her to tell you her story in her own way. I hardly know anything about it myself." He then sat in silence till she brought in a tray and passed three cups of strong brown tea. Charlie guessed this was how Rupert liked it. Charlie was glad when the fragile woman started straight in with a sentence she had probably prepared in the kitchen.

"You never heard of my existence as a child because everyone in the house ignored it. Ignored me. Stafford my brother was three, Graham was one. I was four. Stafford had enough of a presence to be noticeable. People chucked my chin when they passed, but essentially I was not there. Anything I know, I know from local people who were 'belowstairs' here, either full-time or just when the house had visitors, such as the seminars. I have no memories of that time.

"When we left Walbrook and went home to Bassetleigh in the North Riding, I began to note that mother was not with us. It took time, this, because she had never taken any notice of us, to speak of. Stafford she did notice from time to time because he was a marketable commodity: being a boy he established the family's position as potential chieftains of a Quarles clan. So Stafford missed his mother, and as the war continued, he speculated that she was no longer alive: he toyed with various causes of death—cancer, air raid, crime of passion, variations which he hardly understood. Our father, if asked, said she was very ill and hurriedly showed us out of the door."

"What sort of man was your father?' asked Charlie.

"Gloomy, tight-lipped, reclusive. Things changed as the war limped on to its end. Stafford was going to be sent away to prep school—that was in 1944, when he was eight. He was excited but frightened, not surprisingly. He asked our father about Graham and me, and he made inquiries about a cheap school for Graham and an equivalent school for girls. There were a few, but they were very unsatisfactory. Putting me there would have been the sign of a very neglectful father. Then the letter came—the letter from my mother."

"Your mother?"

"Yes. The woman no one mentioned. It said she was now in a position to provide me with a home which our father surely would see was more satisfactory than present arrangements. He would also know that custody was almost invariably awarded to the mother by the English courts. She was quite willing to relinquish any claim on Stafford and Graham: they were boys, and better kept with their father, at least in holiday times. But me she wanted with her, and she suggested he bring me to London on such and such a date and hand me over at King's Cross station. It sounds now like a sordid commercial transaction, but I was still too young to understand that.

"So I left my brothers and my father forever, and when Stafford first came to Walbrook as an adult, we met as strangers. He did not know who I was. It seemed best to keep it that way. I had been described to everyone by Rupert's father as 'one of my Fiennes cousins,' and that I accepted. When I was with my mother, I was kept apart from the business of the house. Now and again I would be taken in to be exhibited to soldiers on leave who missed their own little girls. Often I was in the charge of one or other of the 'girls.' Some were rather sweet and protective, some were hard as nails. After a time there was another child in the house, apart from me, called Hazel. I understood she was the child of one of the staff—the resident prostitutes or 'hostesses.' Her mother's name was Rose. Gradually I understood she was also the child of a member of my family. Jokes from my mother when she was in the 'children's annex' as it was called told me that, and frequent jokes told me that Hazel's father was called Tim, and that he was very hard up. Hazel was kind to me, gave me bits of education I didn't get from the local school, and became the nearest I had ever got to a friend."

"Did you support each other, or were you rivals?" Charlie asked.

"Oh, supported. There was no one else, you see. And

she—my mother—was pressuring Hazel, making hints, disgusting suggestions."

"What sort of hints?" asked Rupert after a sharp intake of breath.

"That she was 'nearly ready,' and that there'd been a 'lot of interest' in her."

"Was your mother serious?"

"Never more so. 'The first year always brings in a lot of money,'" she used to say. 'I'm not a bloody joint of meat,' Hazel would reply. But she was scared, she was disgusted at being 'sold off.' We used to talk about it. I hardly remember talking about anything else, at least until she heard about Walbrook."

"Who was *she*?"

"My mother, of course. We never called her anything else."

"And what did she hear about Walbrook?"

"That it was being returned by the government to its rightful owner. We'd heard all about what happened at the beginning of the war, how it had been sold to another branch of the family. I hadn't understood, but Stafford explained as much as he was able. Mum's rejoicing helped as well. I understood that she had possession of something the Fiennes man would very much like to have."

"Was she blackmailing him?"

"I don't know. I don't think she was threatening to use information against him. It was just that she had something, and she needed any price she could get for it to 'tide her over.' Hazel told me that the London business must be in difficulties. We were interested because whatever she had might save us from being 'sold like meat.'"

"This was all happening in the autumn of 1947?" asked Charlie.

"Yes. At some point a price must have been agreed. She was very annoyed when Montague Fiennes insisted she bring 'it' with her if she expected money to be handed over. 'I'm damned if I will,' she said. 'He could say it was a forgery and never hand over the money.' But we heard her talking to one of her best friends, a creepy-looking doctor of some kind, someone we hated, but he knew all about dodgy deals. He said she would have to let Fiennes see what it was he was buying. She agreed reluctantly. Then she said she was going to take us with her, me and Hazel, so that the Quarles side of the family would be strongly represented. The doctor thought it was a good idea. He thought she should also take some kind of bodyguard, some tough who would see that Fiennes obeyed the rules, but she jibbed at that too. 'I'd trust the bodyguard even less than I'd trust Montague Fiennes,' she said.

"The next morning we two passengers put on our most respectable school uniforms, which both said DAMNED GOOD SCHOOL. We were seen off by the doctor, who asked her, 'Have you got it?' and she answered, 'I said I would, didn't I?' which, as Hazel whispered to me, wasn't really an answer at all. It was a grueling trip in those days before motorways. The assignation at Walbrook Manor was for the next day, and she opted to stay for the night in a country inn fifteen miles or so away from our destination. She had a whale of an evening talking to the yokels and sending them up—she thought they didn't catch on, but they did. Hazel talked to a young man a few years older than her, and they got on fine. As we went up to bed, she whispered in my ear, 'He's a motor mechanic.' Before I went to sleep she said, more urgently, 'If the car starts behaving funny and it slows, jump out.' Next morning Hazel said she was ill and wasn't going any farther. We could come back for her. *She* wasn't having any of this until Hazel said, 'I think they've started.' That was really good news for my mother, and after she'd asked a few questions about what it was had started, she agreed to Hazel staying behind at the inn. I was bundled in the back of the car and we started off.

"When we'd driven ten miles or so, the car started hiccuping and making funny noises. 'What is wrong with the car, Mummy?' I asked. 'Oh, it's nothing,' she said. 'There'll be someone at Walbrook who can fix it.' We were on a back road, my mother thinking that was safest, though in fact it made us more conspicuous, and she was lucky we were not noticed. Well, not lucky exactly . . . The car's hiccups turned to coughs and we started downhill. There were a lot of hills. I shoved down the door handle, opened the door, and jumped out. The car continued down, I heard her screaming, and then a splash. I thought, 'Now she'll be all right,' but I started running, afraid of what she'd do to me. I ran and ran. She must have sunk quickly. I never saw or heard anyone running after me. After I'd been going about several hours, I saw a road sign: WALBROOK, 3 MILES. The village and the house, but I knew one was close to the other. I kept on and banged on the servants' door about ten o'clock. There was one servant, engaged by Mr. Fiennes. He let me in, gave me a cup of Bovril to warm me up, and then sent a message to Mr. Fiennes. From then on I was safe."

"Did he have no doubts? Keeping quiet about your story?"

"If he did, he didn't communicate them to me. Would you? Accuse a child of twelve? All I did was run away. He told me once it was like a dream: his first night in the old house, first day as head of the family, a new beginning. And at his door there appears not a selfish harridan such as he had always believed my mother to be, but a child who has just narrowly escaped death. He must have waited to hear word of the car, but none came. It was a dream, a fantasy come true! He began his time as 'lord of the manor' welcoming a defection from the Quarles wing of the family to the Fiennes wing. From that morning on he fed me, clothed me, made sure I was looked after by someone competent and sympathetic. Soon his wife and baby arrived from her parents' home—you," Mary-Elizabeth said, grinning slyly at Rupert, "and we all got on so well. I've had such a happy life, and the life that I faced before, without ever understanding it, would have been a lifetime of prostitution."

"But what about Hazel? We know what she's become, what she is *now*. How did she get from being a feigned invalid in a country pub to being Lady Quarles? Have you talked to each other?"

"We have exchanged words. When she first came here with Stafford, she made sure she got me on one side, made sure I knew that she knew who I was. 'We know each other, and what happened to us. I don't want to hear a single word more about it. I spent six months with a handsome, young car mechanic, and from then on my life's all been upward. I've invented my own family background, but I don't want to hear about it. *Capice?* Stafford knows about my parentage, but I told him nothing about his mother—your mother. It seemed too cruel.' And she stalked off—very sensibly I thought."

Charlie pushed his cup of tea away and stood up, looking at Mary-Elizabeth and Rupert He had a feeling the latter knew what he was going to say.

"I expect I'll have some more questions to ask you, but I think I should tell you now that I'll be repeating your whole story on up the line. I can't see anyone in authority is likely ever to consider any further action involving, for example, prosecution. What is there to justify it? Two young girls being groomed for prostitution by a sex-mad woman who was also your mother. I think we should quite soon put closure and shut the book. But there is the question of what Mrs. Quarles was hoping to sell to Montague Fiennes. Was it something that could incriminate in some way your adoptive father, Ms. Fiennes? Something valuable, unlike most of the middle-ranking pictures and statues that are in the house now? What was it, and did she have it with her in the car?"

Mary-Elizabeth swallowed. "She was my mother, but I feel no respect for her. It would be like her to say she was doing something and then do the opposite. I think she must have realized she couldn't sell something that she was unwilling to let the buyer see before he paid the money. Only she would contemplate an absurd proposition like that."

"And did Montague Fiennes never say anything about what it was?"

"I don't know. There *was* something that made me think and was definitely concerned with my mother. He was in bed in Walbrook, it was a few days before his death, and I think he knew it was coming. He was trying to say—I find this very difficult to talk about, and he wasn't an emotional sort of person, but he wanted to tell me how much I meant to him, and how valuable my work in the house had been. And what he said was, 'I think it must be the same with people as it is with great music. Someone said it took years before a piece of music was really appreciated and understood. Even your silly mother appreciated that. I'm beginning to know how much I owe to you. It's taken time, but I do know how much I'm in your debt.'"

Mary-Elizabeth smiled slowly, with a little girl's pride.

CHAPTER 16

Safe at Last

✳

About three weeks after that, Charlie, busy putting the so-called case to bed with cautious hypotheses, received a phone call from Julie Maddison. It was a good job he didn't pigeonhole people according to their special fields of interest—and a good job he didn't worry about losing a bet.

"Charlie? I bet you're putting a final touch or two to your report on the Haroldswater case."

"Got it in one."

"Did you think of contacting the car museum at Beaulieu?"

"No. And I can tell from your asking that you did."

"Yes. Very cooperative librarian there. Got out and sent me photocopies of advertising material and newspaper reports on the Marsini-Falk, which was one of the luxury jobs you've been considering."

"Yes. I never found out much about it. A car for the elite."

"Exactly. And one of the things it had to offer, along

with makeup bags and drinks cupboards and a barom-
eter, was a safe."

"Ah."

"Yes. Fireproof and waterproof, or so they claimed.
One thing they surely would prioritize with a safe was
that it should be as unostentatious as possible—more
like a sandwich box than somewhere to put your valuables."

"No photographs, of course."

"No. Just the measurements. Could have been ignored
by the divers as being just an old box. The sort of thing
people chuck into canals and ponds. Maybe it's time to
send them down again. Anyway, I'll e-mail everything I've
got. I see a bet coming up trumps for me, don't you?"

"I shall pay up with pleasure—no, with gusto," said
Charlie.

The return of the diving team to Haroldswater did not
cause any great stir in the vicinity. There was no great
vicinity for it to cause a stir in. But Charlie had read and
seen enough of the thirties and forties publicity material
to know that the safe was inconspicuous and could have
been ignored as some modern packaging, particularly if
it had been grown over by aquatic weeds and covered
with beer cans. He invented an excuse to call in on
Forensics every two or three hours, but unsurprisingly,
this did not hurry things up. Eventually the secretary
there said something was going to be brought in, and
by dint of chatting her up at an unusually slow pace for
him, he caught his first glimpse of a smallish box, with
weeds and household rubbish clinging to it.

"That'll be ages before we can open it," said the head

Forensics scientist. "Don't come in every five minutes, Charlie. We'll call you."

"Oh, yeah? When I'm out on a tricky job miles away? I don't think so."

"Okay, we'll call you the day before it seems likely we'll be opening it up. Satisfy you?"

"It'll have to." But Charlie, often with Hargreaves by his side grumbling as only a Yorkshireman can grumble, called in two or three times a day.

"It'll only be another of those bicycle poems," said Hargreaves.

Eventually the message came. "We should be ready to open up tomorrow, about eleven. We've established there's something in there."

"It'll be a poem about the Tour de France," Charlie prophesied to Hargreaves.

They got to Forensics in good time, but were about the only ones there. The scientific people were not interested in a case that was unlikely to result in a prosecution. The head of the department, with two assistants, slowly, incredibly slowly, began to prize up the lid of the safe. Miraculously the hinge still, noisily, opened as a hinged lid should do. Charlie saw paper and thought that for him paper was more exciting than diamonds or rubies could be. There looked to be nine or ten items, neatly arranged in a pile. The assistants, already gloved, began to empty the miniature treasure chest. Charlie first noted that where there were dates, they were in chronological order. The first date was April 1929. Slowly Charlie displaced the note, which came on top of a very short poem in longhand.

Here dead lie we because we did not choose
To live and shame the land from which we sprung.
Life, to be sure, is nothing much to lose;
But young men think it is, and we were young.

The note read:

Dear Mr. Quarles,

At last! A short poem, but it seems to have been ages before I could get the postlude right. Apologies to Mr. Gurney, though knowing my fellow musicians, I shall not be the last to come up with my contribution.

The poem is not yet published and was shown to me by Mr. Housman. When I said it would make a fine song, he grimaced and said nothing. I think he is no musician!

I have been so taken up with my own thoughts, memories of my own losses, that I am loath to leave the subject and my mind tells me I must write something more ambitious—no, not ambitious, but *worthy*—of not just my losses but the thousands, millions of families who suffered similarly through Europe and beyond. If something does result, I shall not only acknowledge your part in its composition, I shall make sure any profit goes to Walbrook and the wonderful work it is doing and will do to prevent any repetition of the appalling slaughter we lived through and which younger and better men died in.

How I hate the Barbarians now rampant in

Germany. Heaven help us if they gain power! They would have me hate my best friends—the great Bruno Walter, the wonderful boy Menuhin—simply because of the silly irrelevance of their race. Will we never learn? You must teach the world!

I enclose a photograph, unposed, more natural I feel.

Yours
E. Elgar.

The photograph showed the composer with a lot of other people, usually of about his age, on some kind of excursion. Elgar looked straight into the camera. His eyes—and they must surely be the reason why this particular snapshot was sent—were trying to be part of a merry event, but they could not disguise the all-pervading bitterness of his later years, when the civilization he had so admired collapsed, leaving the countries of Europe lacking a generation. As Charlie and Hargreaves stared at the wounded glare of the man, the head of Forensics drew from the safe a large manuscript with a title page on the top reading:

DULCE ET DECORUM EST
An Oratorio by Edward Elgar
1931

"What's the market in oratorios?" asked Hargreaves. "Make a packet, will it?"

"Felicity tells me he wrote three. Two were non-starters. This one, with the story attached to it, may break the trend. Who am I to say?" Charlie looked at the manuscript, which had been opened up so music and words could be seen. So far as he could judge, the music, though wavery, could just about be deciphered. "I suspect the music may be less muddled than the man's political grasp. I think the *feeling* is there, and right, even though he was being used and didn't realize it."

"So what happened? What's behind it all?"

"A set of women, all with connections with the Quarles family. We have Stafford's mother, running a brothel, and finding that a much less profitable occupation in peacetime than it was in war. But she had one trump card."

Hargreaves's eyebrows went up, and he gestured to the pile of music paper. Charlie nodded.

"Then there's Timothy Quarles's illegitimate daughter. Hazel was in Walbrook briefly in 1935. Village gossip always gets details wrong. They remembered it as the time of the abdication crisis. I calculate it must have been the Silver Jubilee. If she was born in 1934 or '5, that would make her just about the right age in 1947— to be the sacrificial victim of Stafford's mum."

"Who didn't have any scruples involving a mere child," said Hargreaves, who had quite a good moral vocabulary.

"No. And Hazel didn't have any scruples about involving a child even younger than herself. And so she stays in bed with her mechanic, who had fiddled with the car, and Mary-Elizabeth goes off with some sketchy instructions as to what to do when the car began to crack up."

"She was the luckiest of them, I suppose?"

"She was. Her 'lines fell in pleasant places.' Who wrote that?"

"Haven't the faintest. Who?"

"Shakespeare," said Charlie, bravely but erroneously. Well—it was where Felicity's favorite quotes often came from. "There could be nothing held against Mary-Elizabeth. A twelve-year-old who panics when the car that's carrying her runs out of control? All perfectly natural. In fact I'd say the two who suffered most from Stafford's mother had the right to a bit of retaliation. Don't tell the chief constable I said that."

"What do we do now?"

"Go back to driving licenses and parking offenses. I'll be grateful to. The trivial is always a welcome relief after a big mystery with profound implications."

Charlie marched off, leaving Hargreaves shaking his head. Hargreaves never knew his boss to be content with trivialities for more than two or three days in a row. And the truth was that Hargreaves blessed his luck, the eternal alternation between pettifogging regulations and downright evil. It suited Hargreaves very well indeed.

About the Author

ROBERT BARNARD's most recent novel is *A Stranger in the Family*. Among his many other books are *A Cry from the Dark*, *The Mistress of Alderley*, *The Bones in the Attic*, *A Murder in Mayfair*, *No Place of Safety*, *The Bad Samaritan*, *Dying Flames*, and *A Fall from Grace*. Winner of the prestigious Nero Wolfe Award as well as Anthony, Agatha, and Macavity awards, the eight-time Edgar nominee is a member of Britain's prestigious Detection Club. In 2003, he was honored with the Cartier Diamond Dagger Award for lifetime achievement in mystery writing. He lives with his wife, Louise, in Leeds, England.

Printed in the United States
By Bookmasters